THE LIBRARY

Against Nature

(THE NOTEBOOKS)

TOMAS ESPEDAL

TRANSLATED BY JAMES ANDERSON

LONDON NEW YORK CALCUTTA

Seagull Books, 2022

Originally published in Norwegian as *Imot Naturen*: *notatbøkene*
© Gyldendal Norsk Forlag AS 2011. All rights reserved.

First published in English translation by Seagull Books, 2015
English translation © James Anderson, 2015

This translation has been published
with the financial support of NORLA

ISBN 978 1 8030 9 053 5

Typeset by Seagull Books, Calcutta, India
Printed and bound by WordsWorth India, New Delhi, India

I'm starting to grow old; I don't recognize myself. It has always fascinated me, this image of age—the old man and the young girl. I don't know what it reminds me of, a crime, perhaps, or nature, the brutality and violence of nature, its innocence. You can't tell which is the guilty party, the man sitting in the chair, or the woman seated on him, on his lap, in her black, low-cut party frock.

The white skin and the old face, coarse and creased, resting against the young naked breast.

The firm, pale breasts cupped by a taut bra. A perfect curve. The white curve of the throat and breasts; how good the old face looks against the smooth skin. He rests. He is content. He's sitting in a chair. She's sitting on his lap; he rests his head on her white breast.

They are in company, sitting in a room apart. A small library, softly lit. They hear the sounds of the party through the wall—voices, laughter, the chink of glasses. Her right arm is around his shoulder, pulling him towards her; he presses his mouth to one breast. There's a mirror on the wall. She's tied her hair in a ponytail, a whip that flails when she speaks or walks; the instant he saw her he forgot his own age.

There was no age in that meeting.

Age came afterwards, when they withdrew and hid themselves in the room with the books and the mirror.

She sits on his lap; he clutches her as if she's his mother. They see themselves in the mirror. It reminds me of a picture, a painting by Velázquez—the young girl seems more beautiful when you see her with a cripple.

The moment he saw her, he forgot his own age. She walked past him as he was sitting surrounded by friends and acquaintances, authors and students, her hair was caught up in a ponytail that beat against her back and shoulders as she clicked past in high-heeled shoes; she was taller than him. He rose, almost involuntarily, and followed her to where she stood with a group of female friends. Not for a moment did he think about his age. Age came later, as they sat in the library and looked at each other in the mirror. A disturbing picture; those two faces, so alike in all their disparity, like two siblings, like a father and daughter, or a mother and son, and perhaps it was this unnaturalness, the grotesqueness and charm of it, the very timelessness of the image, in the mirror, which made them unwilling to let each other go, they were unwilling to let each other go.

He is forty-eight, he seems older, his hair is grey at the temples, a grey, close-cropped beard. A wide mouth, thick lips, there are cuts in the lips and scars around the mouth from fights or injuries, his face is coarse and lined. It's a face that could have been ruined by loneliness or too many pleasures, it isn't possible to say what there is in his face, but it's the destruction that gives him his beauty; she thinks he has a ruined and beautiful face. When she looks at him, up-close, as she sits over him and leans forward to kiss him, all she feels is fear. And it must be a fear she needs, because she presses her lips to his and pushes her tongue into the open mouth. What does she want? Perhaps simply that he should be her lover. Perhaps she wants to hurl herself into something dangerous, calamitous, that will alter her completely. He's sitting in the chair at the desk wearing a black suit and white shirt, a black tie loosened at the collar; she's sitting on his lap, as if they're both familiar with the image that awaits them in the mirror—death and the young maiden.

It's New Year's Eve. He looks at his watch, it's ten past eleven. They hear the sounds of the party in the flat; he reaches out for the bottle on the desk, gives it a shake and eases up the cork that flies out and hits the ceiling, there's a pop; she jumps, gives a start and a shout, the spume catches her throat. She blushes and hides her face in her hands, but he's seen how the blood rushed to her face. He pours champagne into the two glasses, takes one of them and puts it to her mouth and tips the liquid in between her lips, she can't swallow it all and bubbles come out of her mouth, he kisses her.

You're choking me, she says.

He laughs.

Give me some champagne, he says.

She picks up the full glass and pours the liquid into his mouth, she pours as quickly as she can, but he swallows it and she takes the bottle and puts it to his mouth, he gulps and gulps, like a drain, she thinks.

They drink, taking pulls from the bottle. He produces a mask from the pocket of his jacket, a black fabric mask with two small holes in the material that covers his forehead and most of his face, only his nose and mouth are visible beneath the blue eyes. He gazes at her, and now she notices that his look is old. It's as if these two eyes have always been there, in the dark, hanging suspended in the air, without a face, without hands, two eyes that will never relinquish her, that she will never escape; are they a part of her, is this her own gaze that is suspended before her, two staring, oval organs firmly attached to her body, and which have taken root outside herself, like an artificial finger, the extension of an arm; she shuts her eyes. I'm sorry, she says.

He pulls off his tie, winds it twice around her head and hair. A secure blindfold, as if he instantly understands her, that desire for darkness, the absence of eyes; she throws her arms around his head and pulls him towards her.

He gets up from his chair, leaving her to sit in the dark. He pulls a book from one of the shelves, pretends to quote from it: Ovid said that blindness increases the sensitivity of the hands, he says. He takes a packet from his inner pocket, a transparent plastic bag, he sprinkles the white powder in two lines on a sheet of paper on the desk, holds a thin tube to her nostril: Inhale, he says. He forces her head down towards the desk, and cautiously she breathes in through her nose, recalling suddenly being pushed down into the snow, how the snow filled her mouth and nose, that cold snow, she breathes in and is surprised at how hot it is, it burns her nostrils and head, a flame of snow. She opens her mouth wanting to spit out the heat that fills her throat and chest. She spits in his face.

He pushes her head back, and she arches her torso against the desk. Then he pulls her dress down from her shoulders, draws her bra downwards and sprinkles a line of the powder between her breasts. He places the tube between the white breasts and inhales sharply.

There's sweat on her brow, small beads of sweat, they run down the sides of her nostrils, a thin, damp membrane of sweat in the fair down above her mouth; he kisses her.

You kiss like a serpent, she says.

You've got a serpent's tongue.

She sticks her tongue into his mouth, and he penetrates her gently; an unbreakable ring, as when snake bites tail of snake and has its tail bitten in return, as when he lies on the floor and she sits over him; she bends down and puts his member in her mouth while he sticks out his tongue and licks hers.

She forms her lips into a pout and encompasses his penis, she sucks it hard. She makes a ring of her thumb and middle finger around his shaft and moves the tight finger-circle up and down, slowly and quickly, a fluctuating rhythm holding her mouth open above the tip of his penis which she moistens with her tongue. She stretches her tongue out.

He grabs her by the ponytail, and pulls back her head so hard that she has to rise on all fours. She crouches there like an animal on her knees and elbows with her dress pulled up above her hips, and he's an animal penetrating her from behind as she crawls across the floor. She crawls blindly towards the desk, grasps the edge of it with both hands and hauls herself up. A desk lamp, she overturns it. Pens and sheets of paper, she thrusts them away, she leans back against the desk and lifts up her dress.

In his long autobiographical letter of 1132, *The Story of My Misfortunes*, Peter Abélard writes: 'In Paris there lived a young girl whose name was Héloïse. She was the niece of a canon called Fulbert who, out of love for her, had spared no expense to equip her with as much learning as possible. She was rather pretty and had an excellent grasp of her texts.' Héloïse was sixteen. She was twenty-two years younger than Abélard her teacher, with whom she fell in love; he says in the letter: 'So famous and handsome was I, that I feared no rebuff from anyone I favoured with my love.' The self-assured, arrogant and temperamental Abélard had gone to Paris to study philosophy, and to write books; he wanted to be a writer. He taught, and wrote a number of works on logic, but it is largely the autobiographical letter in which he tells of his relationship with Héloïse, that has given him his place in literary history: 'Under the pre-text of studying we gave ourselves entirely up to love, and our studies provided us with the opportunity to withdraw to little-used rooms, as love requires.'

'What more is there to say? In our desire we neglected not a single one of love's pleasures, and if our passion could devise anything particularly stimulating, we prac-tised it, and the less experience we had of such amorous joys, the more intensely we worked at them, and these pleasures never diminished.'

The room, unfrequented, a library with a deep red wall covering which glints when light from the window strikes the silver roses embroidered on the dark material. A leaded window with a wide ledge on which one can sit and read, where Héloïse sits reading. Bookshelves, leather book spines lining the walls, from floor to ceiling. Brass plates with candles in holders, a square mirror framed in rhomboid-shaped bronze. An upholstered bench covered with oriental cushions, the cushions reflecting the same pattern as the rugs on the floor, layer upon layer in a thick covering which gives sound-lessly as one crosses the floor, as Abélard crosses the

floor, closing the door behind him. He stands in the
half-light behind the almost-chest-high writing desk;
he wears a tight-fitting moss-green hose the feet of
which are thrust into his pointed leather shoes. A white
shirt. A tunic of orange velvet tied at the waist with a
thin leather belt. A silver knife in the belt, a pink purse
and a small perfume bottle corked with a golden heart;
he's unshaven and on his head is a round, black hat,
pulled down over the dark, long hair. Héloïse sits in the
window seat reading. She's wearing a black chemise
with a white neck band, an orange-coloured dress with
long arms and an embroidered breast which descends
to her midriff where the thick material is caught up by
a long belt with red tassels at the ends. A hair grip in
the sandy-coloured hair that hangs loose over her shoulders; Héloïse reads and does not lift her eyes from her
book: Glossuale super Porphyrium, Logica nostrorum
petitione sucirum. Is she blushing? Abélard removes
his tunic, his white shirt is open at the chest; he holds
out a piece of jewellery, it's a present for her, for Héloïse,
a silver necklace, a silver serpent biting its own tail.

Abélard places the bauble around Héloïse's neck, fastens
the clasp at the back and kisses her on the mouth—he

who gives a present expects something in return, what is it he wants from her; cautiously she gives him her tongue.

She has never kissed anyone before. She cranes her neck, clenches one hand into a claw. Forcing her long nails into the palm until the skin gives way and breaks.

She lifts her chin and sees how he holds his face above hers; the eyes, the nose, the mouth, the face, it fills her whole field of vision and she wants to push him away. She kisses. She pushes him away from her and sees that she's stained his cheek red with the blood from her hand.

He is her teacher, a man she looks up to and respects. He is Petrus Abaelardus, the author of books on logic and philosophy, clerk and lecturer at l'École du Cloistre, the most important seat of learning in Paris. He is thirty-eight, ambitious and self-assured, they say, and rather good looking, she thinks, certainly not conceited and arrogant, not pompous, as she's been told, but headstrong and wild, as if he's lived closer to nature than to books, closer to the forests than to the universities, closer to animals than to men; and does she not recognize herself in this loneliness? His hair hangs loose over his thin face, only partly concealing his large ears; he has a restless gaze, two quick eyes that follow her with attentiveness and devotion, doesn't his outward manner remind her of dogs, of horses, his way of walking, and bridling, as if he never rests, is always on the alert. She has a closer bond with animals than with people, with her dog and with her horse. Every day, after school hours, she walks her dog across the fields and through the forest; hasn't she fantasized about him, waited for him? He has a sensual and beautiful face, she thinks; don't people say that he spends all his money on entertainments and women? Hasn't she been warned about him, shouldn't she be wary of him? Hasn't she heard that he's fond of girls, that he seduces women? Hasn't she been told that he's written songs and poems about it, about how much he likes girls, his songs are sung in the streets—Lai des Pucelles. The young girls' song.

Isn't she one of these young girls herself? What does she want with him? She tries to keep him at a distance, but then, excited and enraptured, he comes into the room where she sits reading, yes, he comes just like a dog. He puts his head in her lap, sits at her feet. He pulls off her shoes and stockings and kisses her thighs. She lets him do it.

They go for long walks over the fields and into the forest; is he the one she's been waiting for, no, she's been waiting for a boy who understands and loves her. A boy who understands her distinctiveness, her loneliness and stillness. She's been waiting for a boy who's like her, a brother almost, but perhaps this boy doesn't exist, not in Paris, not in the whole of France; she dreams of travelling, visiting other lands, she's begun to read books. She reads in the mornings and in the evenings. In the afternoons she rides her horse over the fields and into the forest; sometimes she lets the dog run behind, the greyhound, the fleet, long-legged Perceval who follows her everywhere. She'd been waiting for a boy, now she walks by the side of a man, who could be her father, and she's decided to give herself to him.

Lily of the valley. Vernal squill. White anemone. Larkspur. Butterfly orchis. Creeping buttercup. Glacier crowfoot. Buttercup. Cress and lady's slipper.

.

Daffodils, yellow and white. Pinks and clover. And in the garden: snowdrops and crocus.

And in the garden:	an oak tree
A pond	
water lilies	
and carp	
narrow, trampled paths	Lime trees
criss-crossing among the trees	Elm and birch
between the flowerbed	roses and bushes
hips and	hawthorn

From a little rise	Notre Dame
on the edge of the park	the cathedral
The sounds, the sound	Church bells
of trumpets	Musicians in
bagpipes and lute	Rue des Menestrels
harp and song	Lai des Pucelles

They walk in the garden. Side by side in the park, the tall, long-haired Abélard and the young Héloïse who holds him on an invisible leash, a strange fetter firm about his neck; the wind occasionally blowing his dark mane across his face and hiding his large eyes, his gaze is restless and acute, a pair of blue eyes that follow her with attentiveness and devotion, he really does resemble one of her dogs. The way he tosses his head and shakes the hair away from his face. Then he looks at her to see which way she wants to go, he follows her movements and her whims, and he's attuned to the least change in her voice, in her mood, as if expecting that she'll suddenly call him or tell him to sit.

They sit in the shade of the linden. Abélard unfastens the blue mantle at his throat and spreads it out like a rug on the ground. Then he opens one of the books they've brought along, as if the instruction is to continue here, in the park, beneath the tree; the teacher and his pupil; he opens the book and reads aloud from Ovid:

But the veteran will love you little by little and wisely,

and he will endure as no recruit can endure.

Yes, he will burn with a smouldering flame, like hay that is damp or a newly felled tree, cut down on a hillside.

This is a more dependable love, all else is short and intense.

The fruit spoils so quickly, hurry and pluck it now!

If you have a face that is comely too, lie down on your back;

or turn it towards him, if that is more pleasurable.

You who are lovely because your flank is slim and long,

Ensure that your neck is bent, as the sheet is pressed by the knees.

If you have supple thighs as well as a perfect bosom,

occupy the edge of a bed directly before a standing man.

Venus has a thousand games; and you play the least tiring of all

when you have laid your body next to his.

If you have an orgasm, feel that you are enjoying it right down to your marrow,

the man must not derive more pleasure from the act than you.

Allow your seductive sighs and your languishing whispers free rein;

in the midst of love-making you must suppress bolder words directly.

Then write upon each trophy: I LEARNT IT ALL FROM OVID.

From where they sit under the great, sheltering lime tree with its crown so broad and heavy that it resembles a house, a hiding place, they can see where Héloïse's uncle lives; they're waiting for him to blow out the candles and go up the stairs to his bedroom on the top floor, then they will emerge from their hiding place and return to the house, and lock themselves in the library. Héloïse will undress, she will stand naked before Abélard. She wants to surprise him. She wants to show that she's not just an ignorant, inexperienced girl, that she's something more than just his pupil; a young girl who's waiting to be inveigled, by a seducer, she wants something more; she wants to strip him of his power, prove herself braver and stronger than him. Such is Héloïse. She sits on the floor, pulling off her stockings. She undoes the belt of her dress and parts the material, clumsily, she's never undressed for anyone before. She pulls the chemise over her head, it catches in her hair, she pulls it loose, tries to hurry, it must happen quickly; she wants to crawl out of her clothes, crawl across the floor and throw her arms around his legs. She wants to topple him to the floor. She wants to crawl over him, and she wants to become someone else.

Héloïse has lost all sense of how she ought to behave, she practically throws herself at Abélard, pulls him to the floor and straddles him as if they're two boys fighting. She presses him to the ground, pins his hands to the floor. She kisses his face and licks it. She bites his lip. She bites his cheek. She pants in his ear, shouts his name in his ear, she whips his face with her hair. She stops his mouth hard with her hand and takes his breath away. She rides above him the way she's imagined that one day she'd ride a boy, a man, a beast; she grasps his long hair with both her hands and rides him as if were a horse, and she's howling and shouting when suddenly she's thrown into the air; she comes down and falls, rolls over and is hurled into a wall that crushes her youth.

It's New Year's Eve. They're sitting next to each other in the library. He looks at his watch, it's almost midnight. She places one arm on his shoulder, pulls him towards her; he rests his head against her naked breast.

I love you, he says.

It's too early to say that sort of thing. I don't like you talking nonsense, she says.

You're the most beautiful girl I've ever met.

I'm sure you've said that before, she says.

Yes, I have, but that doesn't mean it isn't true.

How many girlfriends have you had? she asks.

He shrugs his shoulders.

Three, he says. Or four, maybe more, it depends on what you mean by girlfriends. I've never loved anyone before, not seriously, I've been in love, but I haven't loved.

Never?

Never.

Then you're certainly incapable of loving anyone, she says.

Loving isn't all that easy, he says. How many lovers have you had?

She blushes, for the second time, and suddenly it occurs to him that she's never made love to anyone before, that perhaps she's never had a lover.

I'd rather not say, she says.

Have there been that many? he says.

But now she hits out at him, she hits out blindly, at thin air; he ducks and grabs her hands.

Sorry, he says. I'll stop being silly. Let's go out and join the others.

Already they can hear the New Year rockets hissing over the roofs of the houses. He takes off his mask, loosens the tie that he fastened over her eyes. She stands up and nearly loses her balance, staggers, is about to fall. He runs forward to support her.

Is everything all right? he asks.

I stood up too quickly, the sudden light. I faint so easily, she says.

All at once he feels acutely tender towards her, holds her, feels her trembling, he runs his hand through her hair, kisses her cheek, as if she's already his girlfriend, his closest and most beloved, it happened so quickly, so unexpectedly and powerfully, he didn't know how much he yearned for her, how much he needed her.

They stand on the patio with a view across the city, watching the rockets and fireworks from the city centre and the higher ground around it; he doesn't want to let her go, clasps her firmly in the cold and dark of the patio where they're surrounded by friends, all embracing and kissing, toasting and wishing one another a happy New Year.

Happy New Year, he says.

I can't see you again, she says.

They're standing on the patio watching the New Year rockets blazing and dying in the sky. Watching the New Year being launched, shooting out like flaming stars in crackling bursts that fall and fade. How everything is extinguished and ended in the same moment that it began—a few minutes ago he was young, now he's become old suddenly, he's assumed his rightful age.

He looks around quickly to see if anyone has noticed, how old he is, how old he's become. He has never, for a single year, for the tiniest second, felt different from any of his friends, now he sees clearly and plainly that he's older than them, he sees it in this New Year's light, in this termination that has come so suddenly and unexpectedly, so undeservedly and evilly, in a flash, as when

23

someone opens a door and inadvertently exposes a mirror that reveals the intruder's face: I can't see you again.

His face crumples. His back assumes a slight stoop, and he stands hunched forward with heavy hands. His mouth is loose, half open, as if his chin has loosened from his jaw, he finds it hard to speak, to formulate the words, he doesn't know what to say. His eyes are watery and dull, his brow is sweaty and his hair is damp with it, his shirt is sticky across his chest and under his arms, he fumbles with the buttons of his jacket and attempts to light a cigarette, how his hand shakes! He hears the laughter and good wishes all about him, he can barely stand upright. He would like to fall. Fall head first on to the concrete floor. Smash his head and teeth on the floor, he wants her to feel sorry for him. He loses his equilibrium and is overwhelmed by a sudden feeling of shame, a tremendous anger, he tears himself away from her, pushes past the people on the patio and walks quickly into the living room where loud music is playing, there are people dancing, there are people standing around the walls drinking, some are sitting on the sofa smoking, some are standing and sitting in the kitchen talking, some are lurching around the flat shouting; he's had enough, enough of the party and the noise, enough of youth and stupidity, he's had enough and wants to get home, out and home, he goes out into the hall and searches for his overcoat among all the outer garments lying in a pile on the floor. He puts on his glasses, bends down and searches through the clothes, finds his overcoat and bag and scarf, winds it around his neck and is just about to remove his glasses, when she's standing there in front of him in the narrow corridor.

I'm sorry, she says.

And at this sorry he begins to cry uncontrollably, as if something tremendously hard has dissolved somewhere inside him and is now streaming out of his eyes, he can't stop it, hide it, his glasses magnify his eyes and his tears, and it must look as if his entire face is crying, that it's nothing but a sponge with two brimming eyes full of the water that's pouring out of him.

She smiles. Lowers her gaze.

I didn't mean to say what I did, it just came out, I got frightened suddenly, a bit late perhaps, I should have stopped you, and myself, when we were in the room, but I couldn't; she takes a deep breath and lets it out in a sigh, I didn't want to, she says.

They walk together through the city; into the stream of faces and arms and feet that stagger and walk towards the city centre, there to form a mass of humanity circulating in a pool of rubbish and noise; it starts to snow, light, white flakes that catch the gleam from the street lamps, before the snow forms a white carpet to be trampled and sullied by boots and car tyres, the movements of the city; they go up the steps towards St John's Church, past the house in Vestre Torggate, up the steps and under the trees, through the archway and down towards the bridge, hand in hand across the bridge and down, round the corner towards the street I know so well, Michael Krohnsgate. We walk past St Mark's Church and along the pavement between the brick facades on each side of the narrow, long street that once contained workers' homes but is now filled with student flats, where once there were shipyards and machine shops, and now there are large, derelict areas of dilapidated sheds and empty halls; they stand by the water like hollow shells, you can still see where there used to be ramps and cranes, rails on which ships were hauled ashore, before the normal work was begun: welding halls and workshops for engines and hulls. We walk past the brick houses and the first entrances, No.

57 and 55 and 53, No. 51 where Janne stops and gets out the keys to the street door. We go up the stairs to the second floor, unlock the door of the small flat with its living room, bedroom, kitchen and bathroom. There is a light brown sofa under the window in the living room, a small table, a television and bookshelves, books ranged on the shelves and lying on the table and the chairs, on the floor and on the windowsill, on the bedside table and on the bed, a double bed, beneath the bedroom window, clothes cupboards on the opposite wall. A writing table, a lamp. The usual writing materials, white paper, notebooks. Pens and pencils. A knitted cardigan hung over the back of the chair. A door leading to the kitchen which has a view of the harbour. The kitchen table and those two chairs, the window facing the sea; I've been here before, on the other side of the street, one floor up, the same kitchen, the same view. The view of the harbour and the shipyard and everything that's so closely welded to my past.

WORK, THE FACTORY

I realized very early on that I didn't want to work. Aged sixteen, I got a job in a factory; it was cleaning and oiling the looms in the textile works where my father was a manager. At sixteen I was ready to follow my father, and his father before him, I wanted to be a good worker, a good husband, and later on a good father, like all the fathers in my family.

Just a few months on, and all this lay in ruins—I didn't want to work, and I wasn't going to get married, ever, and I didn't want children, at any price, I wanted to be free.

That summer, it must have been the summer of 1977, was hot, I recall it as a hot summer, perhaps it

31

was a cool and rainy summer, but inside the factory it was always hot, hot and bright. The absence of sunlight was made up for by more than a hundred powerful lamps, they were turned on at seven in the morning, and the large square room with its concrete floor was bathed in sunlight, or so it seemed. A warm and lovely light, streaming down from the ceiling. Down from the long fluorescent tubes that criss-crossed the vault of the roof. A sudden and strong light, they turned it on, and for those of us already at our places on the factory floor, it felt as if the day had just begun. The day began with this light.

We awoke in the dark, or in the grey of dawn, the first light appeared, but still we moved about the dark house in a daze, it was hard to come to. It was hard to get out of bed, it was as if the night hadn't ended, as if something inside us hadn't finished dreaming, something that wasn't rested, we woke up and were tired.

It was five or six in the morning, it was impossible to think, it was impossible to dream, it was impossible to do anything except follow the routine which, half-asleep, would slowly and inexorably lead us to the factory; we were machines before we got to our machines.

We awoke automatically, half an hour before the alarm clock, as if something, a siren or some metallic noise, had pierced the room, we were woken by this sound which was a part of our work, of our dreams and of our sleep, it was a part of our bodies that woke up suddenly to the soundless chime which came from deep within us.

A high-pitched, clear sound, almost like a silver bell.

Quickly, we sat up in bed. We sat upright, for several minutes, perhaps, staring out into thin air. It was hard to remember who we were and where we were going. For several minutes we were no one, and we knew nothing. We sat up in bed without knowing who we were or where we were, if we were animals or men, men or machines. We knew nothing.

This lasted for a few minutes or a few seconds. We sat in bed not knowing who we were or where we were supposed to be going, we wanted to lay our heads back down on the pillow, pull the duvet back up, go to sleep again, that lovely sleep, we wanted to slip back into darkness, on the soft pillows, and just at the instant our heads were about to give way, were about to fall, we remembered that this was impossible; a cord from our necks stretched down to our shoulders and out to our arms, through our spinal columns and hips and on down to our legs, and this cord was tightened by a mechanism that held our torsos and heads up, that drew our legs to the floor and raised our arms above our heads, and just as we stood erect on the floor and stretched our arms in the air, we remembered, all at once, who we were and where we were going—we were going to work.

The time was six a.m., and we dressed with the same movements as yesterday. The clothes lay in a pile on the floor, always the same clothes, working clothes. Our clothes waited for us, they held our shapes and movements, it was just a case of putting them on and following wherever they wanted to go.

Down to the kitchen. Half blindly down the stairs. Eleven treads, they were ingrained in the feet. Out to the kitchen, on with the light. Start the coffee-maker. Sit down at the kitchen table, light a cigarette. At sixteen you did the same as your father and his father before him, you sat in the kitchen with a coffee cup and a cigarette, staring vacantly out of the window.

You're working.

For the third week, six more weeks to go, thirty-five working days, you've begun crossing the days off the calendar, a thick, black line you draw through Monday and all the summer weekdays, June, July, August. Away with the days, one after the other. When all the days are gone, you'll get paid a certain amount. It's the money you're working for. You'll receive your money in cash, the whole lot, in your hand, in Sverre Nordanger's office, on your final working day, that's the agreement. That's what you're working for, this sum of money. These banknotes that are yours and which you'll stuff into an envelope. You'll place the envelope in the inside pocket of your jacket, walk around with the money in your pocket for several days.

What will you use the money for?

Nothing. You won't use the money for anything.

You don't intend to part with something you've worked so hard for easily. You want to keep the money. It will be hard to use this money, spend it, it's already obvious that the money won't give you any pleasure.

At sixteen you sit in the kitchen and get ready for another day at work. You eat a hurried breakfast, make a goodly pile of sandwiches, pour newly filtered coffee into a thermos. You put on your boots and jacket, creep out of the door, shutting it carefully behind you, and leave the house. I wheel the bike down the gravel path, through the gate, ride past the bus shelter where five or six people, the same people as yesterday, stand in line waiting for the bus. I ride down the gradients from Øyjordsveien, at top speed now, past the football pitches and through the grounds of the Business College, quiet, empty, bereft of students, boys and girls on holiday, in the Mediterranean presumably, on the beach, already, no, at parties, still, partying, celebrating youth, celebrating summer, partying and dancing, drinking and making love, and I cycle past the rhododendron bushes and roses in full bloom, lilac, pink, red. Blue sky. Cold, clear morning air, a sudden glimpse of sea, of the harbour and city behind it, a thin mauve curtain of exhaust above the shining bay that disappears behind timber buildings and warehouses, salt stores and fish oil tanks. The row of trees where the birds perch, their boisterous singing which began with the first gleams of light and which slowly quietens as the day begins; I see and hear

nothing of this, I concentrate on my cycling and the
speed, pedalling with all my strength, round and round,
working the gears and the brakes, pushing hard on the
pedals again, tautening the chain and setting the wheels
and the bicycle spinning along, then turning out into
the traffic at Sandviksbodene, a long and almost sta-
tionary queue of cars and buses which are all heading
the same way—to work.

A little before seven I push my card into the time-
clock. Go upstairs to the second floor of the factory,
open the heavy, grey metal door and find myself
instantly assaulted by the overpowering noise of looms,
which stand in two long rows on the narrow factory
floor, the big windows behind the machines and the lit
office windows in front; that fantastic light in the factory.
It's the same each and every time, every morning, that
fear of going in, the desire to turn back, to retreat, to
go home. The thumping rhythm of the machines and
the bright light from windows and lamps frighten me,
it's like standing on the threshold of a new world, a
perfect and beautiful world which you can never leave;
for a brief moment I stand in the doorway looking into
this hall which has become mine but which each day

feels alien and hard. Then I let go of the door, and it shuts behind me, the only thing to do is go in.

It's a hot summer's day at the beginning of July.

The day starts with the strong sunlight shining obliquely through the windows and mingling with the light from the powerful lamps on the ceiling, a hybrid light, it illuminates the looms and the women behind them, white-clad women with shiny plastic hats or pinned-up hair. Their white faces caught up in threads of all colours, red, pink and gold running this way and that, a gaudy spider's web that holds their faces fast, they're caught up in the threads, in the weave that's spun out of the machines. Good morning, good morning, it's impossible to hear what they're saying, I just see their lips moving, good morning, good morning. I walk in among the looms, retrieve my overalls from near the washbasin where I left them, dirty and black, stained with oil and grease. After a few hours under the machine, my face and hands assume the same dirty colour as my overalls. I switch off the machine, crawl under the loom and lie there with a specially designed knife in one hand and cut away the wool and synthetic threads that have wound themselves thickly around the shaft. With the other I apply a thin layer of oil to the cleaned portion of the machine before greasing all its joints and cogs with a small can that squirts out a viscous, lubricating liquid. It drips onto my face; after a few weeks the skin of my face is ruined. Swollen and red, shiny and greasy, every day, when the maintenance has finished, I have to clean my face with diluted white spirit or paraffin, then plenty of soap and water which I dry off with a dirty towel; after a few weeks my face is ruined. After a couple of months I'm completely broken down, my hands and body ache, my back's stiff, my shoulders and neck hurt, my head throbs, I'm worn out and sleeping badly, but each day I cycle to work and lie under another machine that needs cleaning and oiling; I work hard. I tell myself this isn't necessary, I could cheat and take things easy, it wouldn't make any difference, no one would notice, but something ancient and inbred, something that isn't a part of me forces me on, onto the floor and under the machine, it controls my hands and my will, it makes me work hard, harder than I can bear. It works inside me, obstinate, primordial, this strength of will, this sense of duty which I don't feel and yet adhere to, where does it come from? This strict, inaudible voice that I obey and which drives me on, through the metal door into the bright lights of the hall, and into the darkness beneath the machine.

I lie beneath the machine and work unnecessarily hard, unnecessarily carefully, I don't understand it myself, it's a side of myself I don't know—this pride, precision, this tendency to wear myself out completely. I realize during these months that I'm unsuited for work, or that I'm far too well suited for it; I decide that I never want to work, never want a job. I lie under the machine and watch the time, the large clock that hangs above the door says three minutes to twelve. I crawl out from underneath, go to the basin and mirror, wash my hands and gaze at the face that's no longer mine, that belongs to my work.

At midday the production hall falls silent. It feels unnatural; the machines are switched off and the women leave their posts behind the looms, you can hear their voices, and now I see them, the younger women and the older women, taking off their ear protectors and plastic hats and going through the door in a group, down the stairs and towards the canteen. They sit at their usual tables, in their accustomed places, not mixing with the men, the male production workers and the managers, they sit apart, always in their fixed places; where shall I sit? My father's next to the finance director, Sverre Nordanger, they're friends, and their table includes the general manager and the sales manager and all the other bosses: Dag Rasmussen, Gunnar Bjånesjø, Geir Ingebrigtsen and Hermann Bovitz. I can't sit there, or with the male workers, or the women, this is what it's been like every day; I don't know where to sit, where I belong. I buy a cup of coffee and take my sandwiches outside. I sit at a wooden table in a tin shelter, in the backyard, adjacent to the factory's access road; it's for smokers. We can hear the traffic on Bjørnsonsgate, the noise of the birds in the trees beside the caretaker's house, an old, red timber building where one day I'll have lodgings. But this is impossible to imagine just now, as with so much else in my life; I know nothing about the future. Each day, after work, I cycle out of the rear entrance towards Bjørnsonsgate, follow the narrow street to the intersection at Danmarksplass, turn left and cycle along Michael Krohnsgate, past the brick houses and St Mark's Church and under Puddefjord Bridge, left after the bridge and up the narrow shortcut towards the heights of Frydenbølien; standing, I pump the pedals as I head for Damsgård Manor but halt at the brick building where my girlfriend lives.

I've never known a stranger house, either before or since. The first time I rang the doorbell and was shown in, it was like being confined in a secret world, it was unique, it didn't resemble anything I'd seen before. From the outside it was little more than a large, square brick house with a garage and a fence enclosing a small area around it, no garden; it was as if the inhabitants never left the house, which they didn't, except to go to work or on holiday. It was her father who opened the door to me—a small man with short hair and square glasses, pointed features, he had the face of a fox. His appearance was disquieting, a goblin-like little creature who seemed to have struggled up from the netherworld to indulge in shady activities. It was impossible for me to connect this person and his daughter, with whom I was in love; from that first moment I stopped thinking of him as her father. I thought of him as 'the man who opened the door' or 'the man who was her boss'. He was strong-willed and intractable, but, given his way, he wouldn't interfere in the lives of his wife or children, he gave them almost unlimited freedom. I was asked to come in. He wanted to show me all the rooms straight away, it didn't take more than a few minutes, but it would be many years before I really knew the house. We entered the hall which had an electric fire, it flamed artificially. One day I discovered there was an opening behind the fire, it was one of the places where my girlfriend's father hid his money. He had several such hidey-holes, in the corners of cupboards, nooks in ceilings and floors, under carpets, the places weren't difficult to find once you'd got to know him; he was a simple man. Money wasn't the only thing he hid. It was like searching for a rat's nest or a fox's earth, eventually I'd find the opening and the den behind it, and there they were, packed tight in the darkness, the notes. Banknotes and coins, jewellery and watches, they lived their secret lives in the house. Her father showed me around: Here we have the kitchen. A small television set was mounted above the kitchen table, at first I thought it was a screen he used for keeping an eye on all the rooms in the house, that cameras were installed in the bedrooms, in the bathroom, the living room and the basement, and that we were being spied on, but I never found any concealed cameras, and the television set, which was never on, didn't work. Here we have the dining room. Here are the bedrooms. They were furnished like something in a red-light district with large beds and pink curtains that could be opened and closed with cords. White, shaggy carpets on the floors. Innumerable small lamps with heavy, dark shades. Plastic lilies and roses. Bronze-framed mirrors on the walls, and no sign of childhood in the rooms. Here we have the guest room. Bookshelves, a little library around a large double bed with heaps of pillows; this was to be our room. Our study. Here we have the bathrooms. The staircases between the floors had leather-upholstered banisters and were illuminated by coloured lights, there were lamps and light fittings everywhere, the light emanating from the most unexpected places; it shone so brightly that, winter or spring, I got the feeling it was always summer inside the house.

Each day I cycled from the factory to the house at Laksevåg. I rang the doorbell, and after being shown in by her father, after eating dinner with her parents, we almost ran up the stairs and locked ourselves in the guest room. Her parents didn't disturb us, I never quite understood why, weren't they concerned about what we got up to, two teenagers, we spent all our time working on a type of adult education. She was a fifteen-year-old shop girl and I was a sixteen-year-old factory worker. She took off her trendy clothes and I removed my working clothes. She took off her dress and stockings, kicked off her high-heeled shoes. I pulled off my tee shirt and jeans, and every time she stood half-naked, in the panties and bra that emphasized her firm, round breasts, I lowered my eyes, I didn't dare look at her, it was as if I already had an old man's gaze, as if I was, even then, guilty of some trespass; she was only a year younger than me, but I was much older than her.

Her skin was fair, almost white, her pale breasts were supported by a black bra which moulded them into a perfect curve; I'd never seen anything so beautiful, those white breasts brimming in the black material.

I rested my head between her breasts, it must have been an ancient yearning, older than me; I was happy. I'd never experienced a stronger feeling of happiness about something so natural, that fair curve of naked flesh, a young girl's perfect breasts—it's only later, many years later, that I'm ultimately guilty, that I'm going against nature; I haven't changed in thirty-three years.

I'm the same, exactly the same as then, nothing about me has changed. My face has aged, my body, of course, but that apart, everything's the same as before. I've moved around and travelled, married and had children, I've written books, lost my wife and my mother and most of my friends, but none of this has changed anything in me; I'm exactly the same as I was.

Soon the lunch break was over, half an hour, it only lasted a few minutes, eight or nine minutes, that's what it seemed like. We sat in the tin shelter and smoked. The breaks were short, the working day long. I went inside and back to the machines, lay down under one of the looms and cut away the threads from the shaft. I lubricated the shaft and the rest of the machine parts. Oil dripped on to my face and ruined my skin. Oil and paraffin injured my skin and caused boils; I couldn't help thinking that she'd think I looked ugly, that perhaps she'd call it off, that she'd throw me out of the room, out of the house. The machines thumped and clattered. That pounding rhythm had become a part of my work, of my days, of the summer; I didn't notice the noise until I left the production hall and all was suddenly quiet.

Totally still.

A pure, white silence that hit me as soon as I walked out of the door. And even as I was walking out of the door, I was thinking that soon I'd be going back in through the same door, there'd only be a short interval, insubstantial almost, like a dream, a few absent hours, that was all.

The machines stood in two long lines. I moved and crawled in a zigzag between them, hearing only the thudding of the looms, and the women who occasionally shouted to one another, I couldn't tell what they were saying. Most of the working day they spent in silence, standing behind the looms and adjusting the bobbins, checking the threads, that they were running smoothly and not snagging. They were silent, mechanical ghosts. The women at the machines. It was almost two o'clock. Every day, under the machine, I wrote this letter to you. I wrote it to make the time pass. I carved your name with my knife into the threads wrapped around the shaft, three initials, then I cut the threads away, cut them free and wrote that I've never loved anyone like you and that I'll never love anyone else.

I pulled the severed threads off the shaft with my fingers. Ran my hand over the smooth component. The machine's shaft was clean, I covered it with a thin oil, a thicker oil at the end where it drove the cogs that worked the machine and moved the bobbins around, pushed the shuttle back and forth, selected the threads in predetermined patterns, before they were pushed together in a firm band, a tag or a label. I never understood how the machines worked, how the women worked, what their work or mine achieved; I lay under the machine and wrote to you.

At five to three I crawled out from under the machine, stood up, cramped and stiff, muscles aching, back, I had to stretch, unfold my arms and legs and lift my head so as not to walk stooping over to the basin. I pulled off my overalls, hung them up on a peg, they held my shape, my body, they were waiting for me to return the following day. Off with my visor. Off with my work boots. Then I washed my hands. First with white spirit or paraffin, then with soap, then I rinsed them with clean water and dried my hands on a dirty towel. The same with my face. Paraffin, soap, clean water, a dirty towel.

I washed my ears, nose and mouth, washed my neck and hands, my arms up to the elbows, the right and then the left. Perhaps for an instant the production hall struck me as beautiful, just as I was leaving; the great hall resembled the nave of a church with its big windows and light streaming through into the severe interior.

Occasionally, just before I left, I'd stand by the basin and gaze into the big hall where the machines stood in lines, their shadows casting black patterns on the floor— the white light from the lamps in the ceiling mixing with light from outside, the white and the black; I'd stand by the basin and discover a quiver of joy or pleasure in the harsh room.

I covered my face with the moisturising cream my mother had given me. I didn't know what good it would do, my face was ruined. Ruined by oil and paraffin and soap; I wanted to swap my face for another one. Like a machine part which you replace for another that's new and better.

The sun shone in through the large factory windows. A sharp, white light in the bright hall; I raised my hand and waved to the women behind the machines, opened the door and went out.

I jumped on my bike, set off at top speed down Bjørnsonsgate, turned left at the Danmarksplass intersection, into the street I knew so well—Michael Krohnsgate. I cycled past the building where my grandmother lived alone on the third floor, past the house, directly opposite it, No. 51, where one day, many years later, I would go up the stairs with Janne. It was impossible to know anything of this; I would have vigorously denied the possibility of its ever happening, but I knew nothing about that, I only knew that I wanted to get back as quickly as possible to the girl I loved and with whom I wanted to spend the rest of my life.

LABOUR OF LOVE

I was at a party with my girlfriend when a girl came across and asked me if I'd take her home.

She was very pretty and not in the ordinary way, there was something difficult and ugly in her face which made her especially beautiful and conspicuous; she wasn't like us, she wasn't a normal eighteen-year-old with unexceptional looks.

Her eyes were large and heavy-lidded, which gave her an appearance of being sluggish and indifferent, distant, there was something apathetic and weary about her face which didn't tally with her age. A thin, pale face with dark eyes and a full mouth. Thick, chapped lips, a sharp nose and big ears that were hidden by a thick covering of black hair, this curled in a way that wasn't natural, it was obvious that she spent a lot of time on her appearance. Her clothes, too, were unusual, a white tulle blouse and flared, black mirror velvet pants, black, shiny shoes with high heels, she was tall and slim. She'd already put on her coat, ready to leave, perhaps she was bored, her coat was red with a black collar.

Who was that? Eli asked when we were alone again, distracted, as if the evening had lost its harmony.

Agnete, I replied. I don't know her.

What did she want?

She asked if I'd take her home.

And what did you say?

I said I was with you.

She must have realized that before she asked. Did you want to take her home?

No, don't be silly, she was a nuisance. She could see we were together, who does she think she is, she seemed totally daft.

Didn't you even entertain the thought that you could have gone home with her, perhaps if you'd been alone, if you hadn't been with me?

But I am with you.

But if you hadn't been with me?

But you can't, I said, think about something that's unthinkable.

And it was the truth. It was impossible for me to contemplate anything at all without Eli, or a future without her, and yet I married Agnete, it was years later, it was twelve years later that I married Agnete.

We were married in a small chapel, Hestad Chapel in Viksdal, the tiny nave was filled to bursting with guests; I didn't know any of them.

The bride was wearing a white dress, she had a string of pearls in her hair. The bridegroom was dressed in a white suit, a flower in his buttonhole, the wedding seemed so innocent and pure; two months later the marriage was annulled.

But we had spotted each other early on—she grew up in the residential blocks at Fagernes, I grew up in the blocks in Skytterveien; we landed up in parallel classes at Hellen School, but one day she vanished; I think I can remember the day the dark-haired girl was gone, there was a gap in the rows where she should have been as we lined up, in classes, in the schoolyard. I know that her parents moved from Fagernes in Sandviken to Fana. She moved from the Fagernes flat to a detached house in Fana; and it was in that house that I lost sight of her.

Until, one day, I found her sitting in the reading room of the library, I knew her at once. That lean face, slightly askew, with its large eyes and heavy eyelids. She had a face that was older than she was. A brooding or melancholy face that gave her a singular beauty, because she was only eighteen. I noticed she was reading Chekhov's play, *The Seagull*.

One evening I saw her on the stage. She was playing Kafka's younger sister, Ottilie, in a play about Franz Kafka; it was a small part, she only had a few lines, but I remember the way she was forced into a large cupboard, and how she was locked inside it, she vanished in there, she was gassed and died inside the cupboard.

From that moment, I think, it was impossible for me not to love her.

She disappeared and popped up again. This was the pattern even before I knew her. She turned up at the party where I was with Eli. She came over while I was alone for a moment, asked me if I'd go home with her. I couldn't do it, I wouldn't, but the manner in which she left me, so demonstrative and theatrical, as if I were the world's greatest fool, pricked me and produced a stitch that bound me fast to her in a way that wasn't good.

So she vanished and didn't appear again until ten years later. It was at the Café Opera. She was home for Christmas, she lived in Rome where she'd trained as an actor. She'd played the lead in an award-winning film and had been interviewed in the Bergen press under the headline 'Film Star in Italy'.

I'd read the story in the newspaper, and here she was, entering the cafe wearing a broad-brimmed, black hat. A red coat with a black collar, a black, fringed miniskirt, black tights and black bootees. A white blouse. She shook the snow from her hat and coat, seated herself on a sofa alone and drank vermouth through a straw.

Was she waiting for someone? No, no one came. She took in the locale. She didn't recognize anyone, not even me. Had she changed? No, she was the same. The same loneliness, though she must certainly have been used to being alone.

I sat watching her for a while before I dared to go across. Congratulations on your film in Italy, I said. She seemed neither surprised nor irritated, not even flattered, she wore that apathetic, somewhat tired expression, it wasn't assumed, it was the way she was, the way I remembered her, distant and unapproachable; it was impossible to tell if she recognized me or not.

The last time I saw you was in a play about Kafka, you played Ottilie, his favourite sister, I remember you studying Chekhov for your drama-school audition, I said. I remember you as a bumptious and insufferable boy, she said. Yes, that was me, I said. And now you're an author, she said. I borrowed your book from the Scandinavian Institute in Rome, they must have had it because it was about Rome, a love story set in Rome, not very original, she said. No, it probably wasn't, I said. Sit down, she said. I should have left but I sat down.

That evening I took her home. We took a taxi, and when the car stopped in front of her parents' house, she jumped out of the back seat where we were sitting, ran round the car and opened the door on my side, gave me a quick peck on the chin and waved: I've got a boyfriend in Italy, she said.

A few days later she was standing on the front steps throwing pebbles up at my kitchen window. I lived alone in a flat in Danmarksplass, I'd moved back from Copenhagen to live with Eli in Kirkegaten. It didn't work out, and now I was living in a flat that belonged to the factory where my father worked. It was a small flat whose windows looked out on to the shipyard in Solheimsviken; a bedroom, a work room, a kitchen and a bathroom. It was a good place to live. I liked living alone.

She was wearing her red coat, and under it she'd concealed a bottle of wine and two lamb chops. Join me for dinner? she called up to me.

She stayed at my flat for three days. It felt like a relief when she went, but after only a few hours I was sprinting out of the flat and up the steps towards the shop where there was a phone box. The following day she returned, she'd brought some books and her toiletries, and this time she stayed for two weeks.

In the middle of January she was due to travel back to Rome. She would finish with her boyfriend, she said. Then I could follow her and move into her flat in Via Natale del Grande.

As soon as she'd left, I missed her.

I didn't want to go. I put it off and put it off.

She wrote saying she'd finished with her lover. That I was letting her down. That I was just like all other men. That I'd promised to come, and now I wasn't coming.

I paced the flat, the streets, the nightspots, waiting for it to pass, the longing, for it to end.

It was now February.

The cold arrived, and the frost, and the ice.

The flat was beautiful, I thought, there was frost on the windowpanes. A blue light in the rooms; I sat at my writing table and wrote.

At the end of the month another letter arrived. From it I understood that she refused to be dumped. She would do the dumping, she would do the walking out. She wouldn't be left. That was how I read the letter. It was over between us.

One morning I took the plane to Copenhagen. I got on the airport bus to Central Station and walked down Istedgade, turned left into Victoriagade, and rang the doorbell of No. 18. I walked up the stairs to the fourth floor, the stairs I'd taken so many times before; Knut stood waiting in the doorway. What on earth, he said, do you want to move back in?

I stayed with Knut, slept in the living room on a mattress. In the evenings we sat in the kitchen discussing what I ought to do. Whenever I had difficulties, whenever I had big decisions to make, I consulted Knut. He was older than me, and wiser, I was completely dependent on him, on his opinions and the advice he gave. I explained the situation; D'you want to or don't you? he asked. I don't want to, I said. Why not? he asked. I'm afraid, I said. What are you afraid of? he asked. And then we began to laugh. We couldn't stop. We sat in the kitchen crying with laughter; What are you afraid of? he repeated. We often laughed like this, every time we touched on something serious, it was one of the best things about Knut, this serious laughter; What are you afraid of? he asked, again and again, I could barely hear him through his tear-choked laughter.

Three days later I was on the plane to Rome. I took a taxi to Via Natale del Grande, found her door and stood outside for a long time before I rang the bell. Then there was her voice, strange and cold, she was speaking Italian. It's me, I said. I don't know you, she said. Agnete, I'm sorry, getting away wasn't as simple as all that. There's been so much for me to organize, I've submitted a new manuscript and . . . Tomas, it's over between us, don't you understand what I'm saying? I broke it off with Paolo, and you promised to come as soon as I'd done it, that was two months ago. I've been alone for two months. She began to cry. You don't know what a situation you put me in, I've never been alone for two months before.

There was a long silence, only the crackling of the intercom.

If you don't open up, I'm going back, I'm going home, I said. Well, what else would you do, you just go home, she said and hung up.

I took in at a guest house in Trastevere, not far from the street where she lived. In the evenings I lay in bed reading, during the day I wandered around her streets, waiting to bump into her, accidentally, and one day I saw her, she was walking rapidly across the Campo de' Fiori in black trousers, black blouse, black shoulder-length hair; she really was gorgeous. But it was too soon, I wanted to wait. I liked being alone in Rome, I liked suffering, it endowed everything around me with a peculiar intensity, a clarity and emphasis which I needed; the city, the streets, the faces, they all imprinted themselves on me with a particular acuteness which was so necessary for my work; I lay in bed in my guest-house room and noted what I'd seen and what I'd thought in my notebooks. I'd begun to write again.

One day I followed her. We walked about Rome like a couple who didn't belong to each other, who didn't know that one day they'd be inseparable. My whole future walked before me in the streets of Rome. She'd go into a butcher's shop, she would stop at the green-grocer's, buy flowers at the market, walk with her long, rapid strides through the city; I tried to imagine that I was walking beside her, that we were shopping at the butcher's together, that we were buying vegetables together, flowers, that we were making dinner together, falling asleep and waking up together; was that what I wanted?

Now she turned up Via Natale del Grande, glanced at the display in a clothes-shop window, someone called out to her, it was the hairdresser, he stood at his door smoking, she waved, crossed the street and stopped in front of her own door. She hunted in her bag for the key, scrabbled in the bag, couldn't find it, and there was something forlorn about her as she stood searching for the key. She began to empty her bag, an address book, documents, a bottle of scent, she had placed the bags of vegetables and meat around her on the pavement, it was one big mess, she upended her bag, a biro, lighter, a packet of tissues. The sight of the tissues did something to me, I felt sorry for her, she emptied her belongings on to the pavement, and then the bunch of keys fell on to the asphalt, making a metallic, nasty sound on the asphalt, she bent down, retrieved the keys, found the right one and was about to put it in the lock when I sprang forward. Agnete, I said.

The flat in Via Natale del Grande—I liked it immediately. A narrow corridor with three doors, a large kitchen with a small kitchen table under the window, it looked out over a backyard, I sat there at night, after she'd gone to sleep, and wrote. Agnete shared the flat with two other actors, Fiamma and Marco; she had the biggest room, a bright, beautiful room with big windows. A double bed, a round table and four chairs, a television, a phone, that was all we had, that was all we needed; we lay in bed and watched television. I wanted, had to learn Italian, and television was the best, the simplest method of learning the language, she said. Perhaps we could translate a play together? Agnete wanted to put something by Pier Paolo Pasolini on in Norway, or something by Natalia Ginzburg on in Norway; she dreamt of doing Italian drama in Norway.

Perhaps that was why she needed me, she wanted to go home. She wasn't getting good jobs in Italy, she wasn't getting enough jobs in Rome, she wanted to work in Norway. In a few months, in six months. But first I had to learn Italian. Quickly. Only a few weeks later we were sitting at the round table translating *Porcile* by Pasolini. We'd seen the piece at a small theatre in Trastevere. I hadn't understood the dialogue at all, but there was a special poetry in the text, a particular rhythm and beauty that I caught immediately. For a time I was completely immersed in Pasolini and watched most of his films at a small institute run by Laura Betti. Here were all the films, all the books, the newspaper articles that Pasolini had written; I went there every day, in the morning, and gradually got to know Laura Betti, who said: Pier Paolo's murder was political, and Moravia wrote that it was an accident, that Pier Paolo was killed by a homosexual lover. We fell out over that article. Moravia betrayed Pier Paolo, Moravia betrayed Italy, she said. One day Agnete and I took the bus to Ostia where Pasolini had got hold of his young lovers, I wanted to see the beach, the place where he was killed. There was a barracks at the top of the beach which housed a collective of old radicals and anarchists; we sat with them in the evening round a fire, and I asked them what they thought of Pasolini. Pier Paolo sold us out, one of them said, I'll never forget that during the student revolt of '68, which I was part of, Pier Paolo wrote in *Corriere della Sera* that he supported the police in their battles with the students, because the police were the sons and daughters of peasants, whereas the students were the sons and daughters of the bourgeoisie. I asked if Pasolini had fallen into a trap, had the fascists arranged the murder and made it look as if he'd been killed by one of his lovers? Of course it was the fascists, Pier Paolo was a karate black belt, he couldn't possibly have been killed by a lone seventeen-year-old.

Agnete and I translated *Porcile* by Pasolini. After that we translated *L'intervista* by Natalia Ginzburg. When we'd finished the translation, Agnete rang Ginzburg and asked if we could see her, she explained that we wanted to produce *L'intervista* in Norway. After a lot of ifs and buts, Ginzburg agreed, and we took the tram to the flat where she lived. It was on the fourth floor of an old mansion block. The door was opened by a maid wearing a black uniform and a white apron, it was obvious that this was to be a sort of audience, an exception; Natalia Ginzburg lived alone and didn't receive visitors.

She sat on a large sofa, surrounded by cats. I was struck by how tiny she was, by how much she resembled my mother: the same close-cropped hair, the stern, suspicious gaze, the same nose, the Semitic profile, I could hardly see any difference between my mother and her. She had the same temperament, was just as excitable, launching into various impulsive diatribes; I realized immediately that this was going to be difficult. The little person on the sofa, the tall figure in high-heeled shoes that was Agnete. We so want to do *L'intervista* in Norway, she said. We've translated it, I'm an actor and I'd really love to play the main character. The main character is small, said Ginzburg. All my women are small, and they aren't like actors, she said. Then she stood up demonstratively. We both understood at once what this was meant to convey; she wasn't more than one metre fifty tall, and maybe she loathed actors, at least tall actors, she only came up to Agnete's neck as she held out her hand. The visit was over. I took her hand. He's an author, Agnete said, he doesn't understand you all that well, he doesn't speak Italian. Ginzburg gave me a long look; he understands more than you think, she said, as Agnete informed me afterwards. We sat in a small bar directly opposite the mansion where Ginzburg lived. Wearing high-heeled shoes was a dreadful mistake, Agnete said. Forget about Ginzburg, she said, we'll get permission for a production from her publisher.

That evening we argued. Maybe Agnete bemoaned going in those high-heeled shoes for a second time. Maybe I told her that she should have done a little research on Ginzburg before we visited her. Maybe it just might have been an advantage to know that she was a left-wing radical and despised the middle classes, so it wasn't a good idea to use make-up and put on her best clothes and a hat and high-heeled shoes, and suddenly Agnete grabbed my camera and slung it with all her strength at my face, it hit me just above the eye and fell to the floor, and lay there. It was the first but not the last time she threw things at me, cups and dishes, glasses and candlesticks, it was dangerous, I tried to explain that to her, but then she forgot again and hurled a candlestick at my chest. Now I had a black eye and a broken rib.

In the mornings we jogged together in Gianicolense Park; one morning when my chest and lungs were hurting, I stopped her and drew her away from the track, I couldn't restrain myself: Do you realize how much strength there is in your assaults, how much damage you do?

It's because the objects you attack with are just like weapons, there's a distance between what you do and the impact you cause, between you and the damage you inflict, between you and what you do.

Supposing you want to hit me with all your strength, with only your hands, what would you go for, my head or my body, how hard would you strike?

She stood tall and looked me in the eyes, was there a hint of contempt in her gaze?

Here I am, your adversary, hit me, I said. She didn't want to. Let's see how hard you can hit. She tapped me gently on the shoulder. That was nothing, I said, I didn't even feel it. You must be able to hit harder than that. She struck, a little harder, at my stomach. Is that all you can do, you're a rotten actor, a failed actor. Now she hit me harder, in the stomach again. You've got to go for my face, I said, harder. She lashed out again, hard, to my body, I laughed, quite honestly, that was nothing, you're nothing, just distance, just play-acting; you've got to be direct, you've got to be honest, you must hit as hard as you want, as hard as you can, what's the hardest you can manage? She hit me again, still with restraint, she wasn't far from tears. You're theatrical, I said, going about in high heels, throwing candlesticks and glasses, theatre, theatre, show me something different, something real, show me what you can do. Now she hit me in the face, with the flat of her hand. You must make a fist, I said. She clenched her hand, struck at my face, I ducked and the blow missed. I hit her in the face gently. She lost control, hit me with all her strength in the mouth. I felt my lip split, blood ran from my mouth. That hurt, I said, but it's a long way off hitting someone with a candlestick. If you really want to beat me, if you want to injure me, you've got to go for my nose, I said. With all your strength, come on. But now she was only crying, and suddenly she set up a real howl, she was screaming right in my face and I felt how her screaming touched something cruel inside me; I was close to knocking her flat.

We suddenly found ourselves in the midst of a kind of Neanderthal drama, she was wailing and I had to use all my restraint not to go for her throat. I just wanted to strangle her, stop her screaming, but I managed to turn my back and began walking away from her, she caught hold of my track-suit top: Don't leave, don't leave me, she whimpered, we were like two animals, I tried to pull myself loose, but she held on and we tugged and tore at each other.

May had come, May in Rome, in the evenings we made love, or watched television, we saw the films of Visconti and Bertolucci, two of the most moving films I've ever seen: Bertolucci's *La Luna* and *La Caduta degli Dei* by Visconti; both were about young men who loved their mothers; I cried and cried watching these films: God, so this is *your* problem, too, said Agnete, you're still struggling with your mother. In the mornings we'd jog in Gianicolense Park. We'd pound up the steps from Trastevere, run as fast as we could through the park, beneath the trees, past the dogs, the walkers, on the hill above the city, in the early morning light. In the mornings I went to the Pasolini Institute. Agnete looked for work in advertising films and television, film productions and plays, I realized now that although she'd worked in films and the theatre, she was, to all practical intents and purposes, unemployed. In the afternoons we translated Pasolini and Ginzburg, we'd begun work on a collection of Ginzburg's short stories, *Le Piccole Virtù*, The Small Virtues. Agnete often said that she wanted to go home, she'd been in Rome for five years, she wanted to go home and work. Occasionally we'd eat with directors and actors, photographers and television types, people who were important to know; I hated it. On the seventeenth of May we were at an Independence Day celebration with Geir Grung at the Norwegian Embassy, in a vast villa where a line of white-clad black waiters stood like some grotesque frieze behind a smorgasbord of Norwegian delicacies: salmon and lobster and crayfish and cured meats and hams and scrambled eggs. We formed a small Independence Day procession and went around the garden, with Truls Øra at the head; Norwegian flags and songs, a short speech, it was almost enough to make me throw up my salmon and scrambled egg, but Agnete was radiant, she shone, wearing a white dress under a black jacket, under a broad-brimmed hat, with her pageboy-cut black hair, her wide mouth and big eyes. Was she happy? She seemed happy. After the party we walked through the smart residential district and happened to pass a gateway with a CCTV camera; Take me here, she said and crowded into the porch, lifted up her dress and turned her back towards me.

There was nothing natural about our love life. She had all these ideas, all these notions about breaking barriers, about not being normal; she couldn't be, wasn't capable of being, normal; I believe she wanted to be normal, I believe she wanted to be natural, in tune with the people and the world around her, but she couldn't manage it, and later, many years later, she would expend all her effort in trying to achieve what she perceived as natural, and it killed her.

In June we moved back home. We moved home to my flat in Edvard Griegsvei. It had been designed for a man who wanted to live alone, now it was refurbished, refurnished and in many ways ruined, it became a flat for two, but less and less to my taste, I was slowly forced out of the flat and in the end had to find an office, a place to work. My workroom had become her work-room, the living room sported a piano, the kitchen and bedroom were completely altered, perhaps for the better, but I'd lost my flat.

Each morning I cycled off to the room I'd rented from the philosopher Arild Haaland, at his mansion in the suburb of Brødretomten. The billiard room, such a lovely room, a workroom. A writing table by the window, bookshelves and a bench to rest on. Here, over a period of three months, I wrote the novel *She and I.* With increasing regularity, Agnete would take the bus and come to visit me in the room where I sat writing. And she began to make improvements here, too, she moved things, hung up curtains. Soon, this room was hers as well, and not just the workroom but gradually Haaland's whole house. She washed his curtains and suggested changes to the living room and the kitchen. One day we had a picnic in his garden with chicken and champagne, we spread a rug near one of the rhododendron bushes, Haaland emerged from his workroom and strolled past us in the garden: Ah ha, so this is where the bourgeoisie disports itself, he said.

My novel was accepted and won an award; I travelled to Oslo to receive the money, and from a phone box near the National Theatre I rang Agnete to tell her that we were no longer poor, and then she told me that she was pregnant. In that moment I had it all, money, a girlfriend, a child. I stood by the phone box in the middle of Oslo and felt the city vanishing; I was lifted from the ground and sailed through the air, over the capital, over the roofs of the houses in Oslofjord, over lakes and forests, mountains and moors, valleys and rivers until, losing height, I landed in Danmarksplass, Bergen.

When I got home, Agnete had begun packing our things in cardboard boxes. We'll have to move, she said. We can't have a child here, in Danmarksplass, in the middle of all this traffic. I've phoned my family in Sunnfjord, we can rent a smallholding at Sagehaugen, it's just past Sande, just before you get to Førde, which has a theatre, the Sogn og Fjordane Theatre, she said. We'll be living in an old farmhouse with a barn and some rough grazing, in the middle of a forest, my brother will move our stuff.

So one Saturday Tor arrived with a van belonging to the Egg Marketing Board; we loaded our things into it, seated ourselves in the front next to Tor and drove off to a place I'd never been to before. We were driving home. I sat in the front seat and thought of Knut and his laughter; What are you afraid of? he'd asked. I sat in the van driving towards a new life on a little farm in Sunnfjord, and now at last I could say it, loud and clear, to myself: I'm afraid of love, Knut.

*

We were going to live closer to nature.

Agnete became plumper, she filled out with each passing month. Her face altered completely; I hardly recognized her, gone was the heaviness and apathy, the tired and distant expression that had characterized it; it disappeared, or rather, it transplanted itself from her face to mine.

We lived in the middle of a big forest. In the past the trees had been cleared to make a large meadow that stretched from the house to the edge of the forest which encircled the smallholding. An old, white house. A hay barn, a storehouse raised on pillars, a small garden behind the house and a stream that ran past the garden and down to the river in the bottom of the valley. The house lay in a hollow, a depression in the forest, shaded, except for a few months in the summer when the sun, alien and strong, shone in through the bedroom window. It was a two-storey house, the kitchen and bathroom, living room and bedroom on the ground floor, two or three smaller rooms upstairs; I can't remember it accurately, I hardly remember the house at all, even though we lived there for two or three years.

The house lay at the end of a narrow gravelled road.

At the other end of the road, at the top, dwelt our nearest neighbour, an eighty-seven-year-old man. It was his road, his property, we were living in his child-hood home. The house was full of old things, old furniture; the curtains and carpets and furniture were just as they'd always been.

Agnete cleaned and cleared, moved the furniture around. She made new curtains. Took up the carpets and painted the bedroom dark blue. We bought a new bed. Some new lamps, an armchair. The house was being made ready for a birth.

We bought half a dozen chickens, they were in the kitchen in a crate. I enclosed a square piece of ground outside the barn with chicken wire. Removed the cobwebs and junk, earth and dust from the raised storeroom, placed a wooden table by the window, a chair, some books on a shelf, a radio-cassette player, ashtrays and two lamps; this was where I would write.

We spent the money I'd won for my novel on a second-hand Citroën, a black CX Pallas, it was a beautiful car, practically a yacht; in the evenings I sat in it smoking cigarettes.

The car was soon ruined, we'd lined the large boot with plastic and used it to ferry the sheep manure we got from Reidar Søgnen, which Agnete used on the garden. She grew carrots and potatoes. Cauliflower and sugar peas. She grew flowers. She made a herb bed. She hammered down some decking to form a kind of terrace, put up corner posts and sewed four sheets together to make a sail that hung over the terrace. She constructed a greenhouse out of old windows and plastic; she grew tomatoes. She baked bread every morning. Bought sides of lamb and pork and beef, cut the meat up and hung it in the larder which was full of flour and maize, sugar and salt, citrons and raisins, everything we needed for the state of emergency that was childbirth.

She wanted to have the baby at home, in the house.

A home delivery, it was natural.

The child was due at the end of May, perhaps in June. Agnete had applied for a job as an actor at the Sogn og Fjordane Theatre, and she got the job, she was to begin in August. She hadn't said anything about the baby. A boy or a girl, we had no idea; I hoped with all my heart it would be a girl. I wouldn't be able to stand being alone in the house with a son.

I sat at the storeroom window with its view of the forest, trying to write; it would be four years before I produced another book.

At the end of May the midwife arrived by plane from Bergen. She was given a room on the first floor, but nothing happened; we went for long walks, we made love as often as we could, but the child didn't come. It wasn't in the right position inside Agnete's womb anyway. With its head up and bottom down, it had been trapped by the pelvis. It would be a breech delivery. Or a Caesarean? The district general hospital at Forde telephoned to say a Caesarean would be necessary. It was a woman doctor. I could hear Agnete shouting down the phone: I'm the one giving birth, she screamed.

But nothing happened. The midwife flew back to Bergen, we were alone in the house. We waited. We waited for the child.

Agnete had told her parents to keep away. She told me that my parents were to keep away. It was her and me and the child. I was to phone the midwife when the time was approaching, when the contractions became more regular, stronger, when her waters broke; I didn't know when I'd ring, the midwife would fly from Bergen. Irene, one of Agnete's friends, would collect her from the airport. We probably hoped that Agnete would see sense. That she'd change her mind. We hoped and believed that at the last moment she'd change her mind, that she'd ask me to drive her to the hospital, or that I'd coerce her into the car and drive her to the hospital. That was what we all hoped and believed. Her parents and my parents and the midwife and Irene and I.

But I said nothing, nothing about all this. I'd read in a book about home confinements that if the man suddenly displayed doubt, if in the midst of it all he began to have qualms and showed these qualms, these fears, this helplessness and impotence, this weakness of his, the woman would never forgive him.

And Agnete lay in bed, she was reading a novel. She was making notes, writing pages of notes in her notebook; what was she writing, did she want to become an author?

She read and wrote. She wrote in the mornings and during the day and occasionally in the middle of the night, she switched on the bedside lamp, sat up in bed and began to write.

Was she frightened of dying?

Was she frightened of giving birth?

Was she frightened of becoming a mother?

What was she writing?

She was an actor, smallholder, gardener, carpenter, mother-to-be, and she was a writer. I was nothing, I was paralysed. The move had happened so quickly, everything had happened so quickly; I spent most of my time trying to catch up with all the things that were stretching out in front of me; the new place, the house, the birth, daily life, the countryside, everything was in flux, it rolled out rapidly in front of me while I sat completely still, trying to make sense of what was happening, where I was, what to do with myself, how I was supposed to fit in. On the fifth of June, early in the morning, the labour began. It was a warm, sunny June morning. The sun shone in through the bedroom window. At one point, in the middle of the birth, I opened the window wide and a bird flew into the room.

It flew round the bedroom while Agnete struggled in labour, tossing this way and that in the bed, crying out and breathing, pushing and sweating while the bird criss-crossed above the bed, from wall to wall, like some benison or special alarm in the room; it was full of light and apprehension and power. I'd phoned the midwife in Bergen, she was on her way, giving instructions on her mobile phone; I spread a plastic sheet on the floor, boiled water and got out the scissors for cutting the umbilical cord. I massaged Agnete, clasped her, stood with her, lay under her in the bed; she wanted to give birth lying down, then standing up, then squatting, I followed her movements, her wishes, her demands, her attempts, she wanted to lie and stand and sit, she wanted to walk about the room, she was searching for the right place and position to give birth. For a few hours I was an inseparable part of her, I held her, she held me, walking, standing, sitting, lying, we were one interlinked body. She had the pangs and the labour and the birth, I had her body around mine, holding tight, two bodies in unison, four arms and four legs that were giving birth to a child.

The child came bottom first, then the legs, they kicked out from the child's body which fell to the floor, on to the plastic sheet where Agnete crouched with her face towards mine and with her arms around my neck, over my shoulders.

The child dropped out, on to the floor. We crouched. My arms around her back. The child fell from her body, still attached by the thin, blood-blue umbilical cord. I leant forward, the placenta came, then I turned the child around, the first thing I looked for was its sex, the child's sex, there was a cleft, and I began to cry, it was a girl.

The child was a girl.

Agnete, it's a girl.

I don't think Agnete was concerned about it being a boy or a girl; she'd given birth to a child. She got back into bed, I placed the child on her chest. It was a girl. A tiny girl child with great, dark eyes. I cut the umbilical cord. The midwife had arrived, she was there in the room with Irene, we'd hardly noticed them at all, now they were in the room with us. I took the placenta out, buried it away from the house, close to the stream. Ten years later I would dig a similar hole in the ground, and stand in exactly the same attitude with a spade in my hands, bent over the hole I'd dug; but then it would be Agnete's urn I was placing in the hole: I covered it with earth, straightened my back and thought back to the moment when I buried the placenta. I straightened my back, carried the spade back to the tool store and returned to the house where Agnete was lying with my daughter in her arms.

*

Three months later Agnete was working full time at the Sogn og Fjordane Theatre. I was alone with my daughter in the house. She woke up early, usually about five o'clock, before it was light; we sat in the kitchen and waited for morning to come.

We sat in the kitchen waiting for the night to end, for the light to come, for the morning to begin.

And the morning came, at last it came, the light came and the sounds of morning and of summer. We lay on a rug in the sun in front of the house, the little baby and me. We didn't miss its mother, it was only when she vanished for good that we missed her.

The theatre was to go on tour, first by bus and later on a boat, in and around Sogn og Fjordane. Agnete insisted that the child come on tour as well; I don't know how she wangled it, perhaps she threatened to leave halfway through rehearsals; it was decided that the child and its father should be included in the tour of Sogn og Fjordane. Doubtless, this was the first time that an actor had been allowed to take the family on tour; we were to stay in hotels all around the county, in Sogndal, Solvorn, Balestrand, Loen, Stryn, Måløy and Florø, and other places I can only recall for their morning darkness; I pushed the pram around their empty streets so that the baby wouldn't disturb the actors sleeping in their hotel rooms.

September, October, the weather was turning cold. The baby woke at five a.m., was breastfed by her mother, dressed and taken out in a pram by her father, out into the dark, out into the cold. We walked the deserted streets of these little places in Sogn og Fjordane. I began to entertain suspicions that Agnete had fallen for one of the other actors but I couldn't face asking her, hadn't the strength to confront her with it; I went out with the pram, morning, noon and night. Sometimes I put the baby in a child carrier, then she'd sit on my back as I clambered up to the peaks and high moors surrounding the places on our itinerary.

At the end of October the production moved into the theatre boat, Innvik. We were given a small cabin in the bowels of the boat. Away from the actors who had their living quarters at the top of the vessel. The cabin was dark and hot, without portholes; it was right next to the engine room and smelt of diesel oil and paraffin. I lay in the bunk with my daughter and heard the noises of the play on the stage right above us; there was singing and shouting and applause. They were performing *The Threepenny Opera* by Bertolt Brecht. The play was full of whores and highwaymen who lived their dissolute lives right above the heads of the child and father who clasped each other and tried to sleep.

In the mornings the boat moved on, to a new place, at the head of the fjord, or in one of its arms; ten or twelve people would come to watch. The actors had begun to tire, they were irritable, unhappy, with hardly any audience; they played to one another, to themselves, they gave way to their own inclinations and weaknesses, the production collapsed, fell apart and bumped along in bits and pieces, it clattered along, piercing and false. I never watched the show, it must have been dreadful, perhaps no theatrical production has ever come closer to Brecht and his world.

Agnete turned political during that Brecht interlude. She'd become a feminist.

What was she reading? She read as never before, book after book, countless books that changed her completely, not just her thinking and language, or the way she spoke and behaved, but also her appearance. She stopped dyeing her hair. She stopped using make-up. She stopped dressing up, gone were the hats and coats and skirts and jewellery; she dressed plainly and simply, in natural colours, natural fabrics. One day when we were out in the car—she was the one who drove the car now——we needed to stop for petrol, and this time I just sat tight; I didn't move and we simply sat there looking at each other. We didn't speak. We simply sat there and looked at each other. I don't think there'd ever been a bigger gulf between us. That silence, emptiness, was it filled with contempt? You're the driver, I said at last, so you've got to do the petrol. She'd never done it before. She got out of the car resolutely, slammed the door, and struggled for a long time to open the cap and select the right pump, put petrol in the tank, she was livid, did everything wrong. I climbed out of the front seat, went into the shop to buy a newspaper. Then she came in to pay. I hadn't noticed before, but there was a collection of girly magazines on display to the left of the till, on the top shelf, above the other magazines. Agnete spotted the magazines at once, she was about to pay, a youth was working the till. Why are those magazines there? she demanded pointing. The boy reddened, shrugged his shoulders. Why are those magazines displayed here, right next to the till where I have to pay, I'm not paying until you remove them, she said. What if I'd brought my daughter in here with me, she'd have had to look at these magazines, too, this denigration of her own sex, and she's only a child. I want to talk to your boss, she said. The youth went out to the back of the premises. I left the shop. Got into the car, into the back seat next to my daughter. It was going to be a difficult drive, a difficult day, perhaps it was the start of everything that went wrong.

After the Brecht tour had ended, just by chance, if such a thing exists, a notice happened to be pinned up on the board at the Sogn og Fjordane Theatre: Actor required to lead a theatre group in Nicaragua. The group consisted of six female actors who performed political drama. The group of women travelled around the villages of Nicaragua, giving their performances in bus stations and shopping centres, anywhere where people gathered. The productions were often improvised and instructional, they questioned the strict, patriarchal role models in Nicaragua. The group needed a leader, financed by Norad, preferably a woman.

Agnete applied for the job and got it.

We were at a funeral when she intimated the importance of us getting married. As a spouse I'd get a monthly income of 12,000 kroner from Norad. As a partner, lover or fellow traveller, I'd have to cover the travel and residential costs myself. We were to spend two years in Nicaragua. So, we had to get married. The deceased had only just been put in the ground when Agnete made contact with the priest. They sat next to each other all through the dinner that followed the funeral. The priest was known for his interest in the theatre. It was agreed that the wedding would take place in Hestad Chapel, in May. I wasn't pleased about having to get married, but I was glad we were to get away from the smallholding in the forest, the house in the hollow, the hard, natural and false life on the land.

Wasn't the life we lived genuine? Weren't we living in the country, surrounded by forest and animals? Hadn't we given birth to a child at home? Yes, but we didn't love each other. We lived together, had a child together, just about cooperated, but the love between us had gone. Perhaps it had never been there at all. Now we were getting married. It was natural. It was as if we were being whirled along on a merry-go-round that we couldn't get off—it spun madly, we clung to each other, now the pole had come adrift from horse and was circling in empty air, and we were shooting straight ahead, out of orbit, at blinding speed, towards a place we knew nothing about.

Nicaragua.

It was a long journey, much further than the actual distance. First we had to attend a two-month course for Norad Peace Corps workers, which was held in Oslo; then we were to spend two months in Guatemala, in Antigua, learning Spanish, before being sent to Managua where there'd be a month's course and preparations to enable us to live alone in our house in the mountain town of Matagalpa.

We left the house in the forest for a small flat in a block at Sognsvann. Two small rooms, a tiny bathroom and a communal kitchen; I loved it, we were suddenly among people, young people, we were in Oslo. We were newly married and we were in Oslo, close to the College of Physical Education and the forests of Nordmarka; I decided to turn over a new leaf. I would begin by losing those 20 excess kilos I'd put on in Sunnfjord, and which I hid behind, like some protective costume, some survival suit made of fat. I was a corpulent, craven author who never wrote a word, who did everything to avoid arguments and confrontations, who used all his energies to take care of and bring up his daughter, but what a father she had to cling to—a fat, cautious, squidgy man who did what he had to and no more. But new times were coming, a time for change, rebellion, revolution, it was time for Nicaragua.

I had to get ready for Nicaragua. Each morning I ran a circuit of Lake Sognsvann. In the lunch break I swam 500 metres in the pool at the College of Physical Education. After the course was over for the day, I walked all the way into Oslo city centre. I bought books at Norli's, went to a cafe and read, made notes. I took the tube home. Sat in the communal lounge with my wife and daughter and the other Peace Corps workers, and their spouses and children. At night I tried to write but couldn't manage anything. My writing had stopped, the words wouldn't come, my voice had gone. I hadn't time to worry about it, soon it would be morning, another day of coursework. There was communal breakfast. Then it was off to playschool with my daughter. A circuit of Sognsvann. Course. Lunch. A visit to the pool or the gym; cycles, weights, punchbag boxing. More classes. A stroll into town, more evenings in the communal lounge. At the weekends there was entertainment and dancing, African dance, Latin American dance, they showed African and South American films; I gave it all a miss and went to bed early. Turned in at the same time as my daughter, lay in bed and read.

Where was Agnete?

She was doing Latin American and African dancing. She had married and experienced marriage as a liberation, she married and became free. I learnt that she was flirting and dancing, that she was behaving outrageously, I ought to take action, they said, weren't we newly weds, with a toddler, weren't we a family heading for Nicaragua? It would be tough, it would be hard, we had to work together, they said, if not we wouldn't manage to live in Nicaragua. We began to argue. There wasn't much room to argue in, two small rooms in a residential block. We shouted and screamed. The sound permeated the walls, it reverberated along the central heating pipes, up and down the various floors. The sound seeped out of the doors, the windows, it resounded in the stairwell and rolled like thunder across the car park in front of the block. One weekend Agnete had had enough, she decided to travel home, home to her parents in Bergen, she needed a rest. I stayed in

Oslo with my daughter. I clung to her. We were a pair, father and daughter. We visited the palace, ate out, took the bus to Huk and bathed in the sea. It was a lovely weekend, a quiet and peaceful weekend. My daughter and I were alike in that we were both quiet and reserved, we lived, each in our own way, in our own worlds; we walked hand in hand away from the beach at Huk, ate a sausage, an ice cream, took the bus and tube back to the flat where I read her Shakespeare in bed, until it was time to go to sleep. It was an idea I had, a desire to read her something that I liked myself, never mind if she didn't understand it; I wanted to read Shakespeare to her, and not the children's books I couldn't bear, and that I couldn't be bothered to read aloud. Later, she told me that my readings from Shakespeare had frightened her, that the graveyard scenes and poisonings, witches and ghosts, swords and knives had given her nightmares, and that my Shakespearian excerpts were the cause of her subsequent resistance to all the books I recommended. She didn't want to read *Wuthering Heights* by Emily Brontë. She didn't want to read *The Bell Jar* by Sylvia Plath. She didn't want to read any of the books I gave her. But as a two-year-old she was defenceless against Shakespeare and my readings; I read *Romeo and Juliet*, *A Midsummer Night's Dream*, *The Tempest*, *Hamlet* and *Macbeth*.

On Sunday we were to fetch Agnete from the airport. We borrowed a car from Norad and drove to Fornebu. As soon as Agnete emerged into the arrivals hall I could see that something had happened to her, something had changed; it was the way she walked, with more gaiety and lightness, she seemed happy. I could tell at once that she'd been with another man. We'd been married for two months, and here she was glowing and contented walking out into arrivals at Fornebu. I don't know what I gave away, whether my face fell, if it darkened, but she saw it immediately and put a finger to her lips, she placed her index finger across her lips as a signal to me to keep quiet and not get upset: We'll talk about it later, she said. We'll talk about it when we get home.

Home.

We had no home. We lived in this marriage, in this union, and now it was ruined. When she finally told me what had happened and how, I walked straight out of the door, ran down the stairs and jogged to the tube station at Sognsvann. A beggar was sitting on the wall outside the supermarket. Dangling his legs, he stretched out a paper cup and shouted something; I stopped, turned, went over to the wall and shoved him in the chest as hard as I could. He toppled backwards off the wall, landed in the bushes, and lay on his back bellowing in the shrubbery. I ran all the way to Majorstuen. From there I got a taxi to Fornebu. Bought a ticket and flew to Bergen. Where should I go? I had a friend who was in town, he was living in his parents' house at Eikeviken. I got the bus to Hellen Skole, walked down the winding road to the house I'd often visited as a child. So this was some kind of return journey; I had to find a fixed point, a starting point, maybe, I didn't know, I was moving through a fog and a chaos, and it had led me to this very place.

Eirik opened the door. Knut was on a visit, how strange, here was Knut who'd asked me what I was afraid of that time I met Agnete. Was I back at the start of this whole story, or was it the conclusion?

A beginning or an end?

The story might have finished here.

We sat in the living room, Eirik, Knut and I. A soft, milky light came through the large window with its view of the sea. There was something surreal about sitting here in this safe sitting room with its old furniture and heavy curtains, like sitting in a dream; I was somewhere else. And yet we were sitting here, around the living-room table, smoking cigarettes and drinking spirits. I remember looking at the curtains and furniture, the paintings on the walls, the lamps, the chairs, the rugs on the floor, a piano, photographs in frames, doors, windows, all this expensive, solid stuff that constitutes a house, a home. I looked at the living room as if I was seeing it for the last time, or as if I was trying to hold on to an impression, a memory.

That night the house burnt down.

We sat talking in the living room; I was full of aggression, there was a fire inside me. I explained what had happened, why I was there, that I oughtn't to be there, that I didn't know where to go. I talked and drank, smoked and drank, raged and drank. I was furious and drunk. You can sleep in the basement room, Eirik said. He shepherded me down the stairs, into a small room, got me to bed. I awoke naked in the garden. Eirik had hauled me out of bed, out of the room, which was full of fumes from the fire, I was insensible.

I lay naked on the grass in front of the house. Someone spread a blanket over me. The house was on fire. I should have been dead. But the crackling of a burning chest of drawers had awoken Eirik, he'd run down to the basement and pulled me out of bed, lugged me out of the house. The fire brigade arrived, they tackled the blaze. I was lifted into one of the fire engines. I lay there feeling guilty—it was my fault the house was on fire.

My clothes were consumed, and my shoes. The bag containing a new manuscript, as well as documents and notebooks, they all went. Money and plane ticket, Visa card and passport, everything went up in smoke.

Was it a beginning or an end? I had nothing; no family, no address, no documents, no clothes, for several hours I was naked.

A few days later I flew back to Oslo. Agnete and I were referred for marriage guidance; I remember the psychologist saying that my wife's infidelity now gave me a certain latitude in our marriage, I could, if I wanted, commence relationships with other women. Several weeks later we took a plane from Oslo to Guatemala City. We flew over New York and Mexico City; it was so odd seeing these huge cities beneath us, all the houses and lights, all the invisible people who were lost in the streets and buildings; they could hardly be seen, and yet there must be thousands of them who had problems like us, thousands who were worse off than us, thousands who were better and worse and just as badly off as us. We sat next to each other in our seats, mother, father and daughter, a small family completely off course, flying in the wrong direction. We should have been flying home. We should have flown directly from Sunnfjord to Bergen but we were making an appalling diversion, across the USA and Mexico and Guatemala and Nicaragua, we were flying right to the other side of the world before we finally arrived home.

From Guatemala City we were taken by bus to Antigua. The bus climbed the twisting road to the old town above; we were coming to help others, to carry out a task in the Peace Corps, but we were embroiled in an internal war, we were the ones who needed help. We needed the help of all those who were unable to help us: the poor and the homeless, the beggars and the thieves, the prostitutes and the soldiers, all the people we were to meet in our hopeless sojourn in Latin America.

In Antigua we were lodged with a family called Gonzales. There were four of them: father, mother and two daughters. They lived in an old farmhouse, just outside the city, to the south-west, just under the foot of the volcano, Volcán de Fuego. The house was divided into three—a main building and two wings which hugged an enclosed garden. The garden had a tree, and a dog was tied to it. A mongrel, Cesare, watched over the house and all our movements, as if we were intruders and unwelcome, as indeed was the case; we were to live with the family for two months. We were given our own room with three beds, a wardrobe, a few chairs, and that was all. There was nowhere to write. We shared a bathroom with the family, and ate every meal with them in the kitchen which had an open hearth. Our daughter had her own nanny, a young Maya Indian girl, Linda, who lived in the house. Agnete had a Spanish teacher; each morning he collected her in a car, and they drove off to the school in the city centre.

I walked around Antigua searching for a place to write. One day I passed a hotel, and it struck me that maybe I could rent a room. I could sit there and write, and if I wanted to, I could spend the night in the room, with a woman perhaps; I was a free man. I had plenty of money.

The money came into my account each month, a regular, monthly payment from Norad. I'd got a grant from the Authors' Association; here, in Guatemala, I was a rich and well-heeled man. I'd never been that before, I'd always been short of money, always been on the margins of poverty, always had to be thrifty, economical, stingy almost. Now suddenly I was rich. I bought a new suit, new boots, a hat and a leather bag which I carried over my shoulder. I walked into the hotel reception. No one there. The hotel seemed empty, deserted. A painting of birds hung behind the desk. A lamp with a green shade, it wasn't lit. An open door and a garden beyond. A man was working there, he was digging in the earth with his hands. He straightened up when I called. A tall, dark-haired man of my own age, his brilliantined hair combed flat and swept back from his forehead. He had a small moustache. I said hello. Told him in English that I was an author, that I was looking for a room in which I could write. He said that the hotel was closed. He'd inherited it, it was going to be renovated. The hotel is empty, he said, but if you want to sit down and write, I can give you a good room, the best room, just next to the garden, a small room with a window, where you'll get a fine view, you can see my flowers.

The very next day I carried my typewriter and books to my hotel room. I bought flowers at the market, a bunch of white lilies, a bunch of white roses. I bought bread and butter, a knife, several bottles of wine, bottles of water and cigarettes. Then I placed the table by the window, pulled the bed up to my writing table, two lamps and a chair; now I had everything I needed.

The room was blue, a deep shade of blue, broken by the white window frame and the light that came through the window. A dark brown wooden floor, a door which I kept open, it gave on to the garden and the flowers there, a cedar tree and a small pond with turtles in it. But what characterized the room most of all was the silence and emptiness around it, all those empty rooms and the quietness of the hotel, the absence of guests—the overpowering feeling of loneliness and decay.

The proprietor, Eduardo Mores, said: I'm a journalist, a political journalist. I'm lucky to be alive. Last week, on my way here from Guatemala City, a car drove up next to mine and they began shooting from the back seat, they smashed my windscreen with their bullets, peppered the tyres. He smiled. We're not all that safe here in the hotel. I'm in and out, I'll give you your own key to the gate and your room. You must remember to lock up. What are you writing? he asked. I'm writing a novel, I lied. What's it about? The novel's about a young Norwegian family who move to Latin America, I said. That's good, he said, I'll tell you stories you can fill up your novel with, it'll become a political novel, he laughed, full of corruption and violence, like Guatemala, he said.

I walked to the hotel each morning after breakfast. Strolled from the family home on the outskirts of town, through the centre of Antigua, across the square and out to the other side of town where the hotel stood in a narrow street that was all my own. Here, there was a cafe, a barber, a small bar frequented by prostitutes. Walking this route was like undergoing a metamorphosis; I was one person when I went out of the door at the Gonzales', and another when I unlocked the gate of the hotel on the other side of town. One evening when I was sitting in this bar, it was crowded with customers, they'd filled the seats around the tables and the space all along the counter, a man entered wearing a hat and poncho, he positioned himself in the middle of the room and began singing at the top of his voice, a tearful, agonized song, he sobbed, he wept, he sang out his suffering with all his strength. Then he produced a trumpet and blew the dregs of the pain and weeping out of his body. I sat there as if paralysed, how dared he, how could he, just come into the bar and stand in the middle of the room, giving vent to his emotions in that way, right in front of every stranger in the place. He blew his trumpet, and I recognized the lie I was living, with all its weakness and cowardice, its silence and caution; I wanted to be like this man with the hat and poncho, I wanted to be a candid and uncompromising person, I wanted to write the way he sang, I wanted to be an honest and difficult man.

I sat in the lovely, quiet hotel room and couldn't write. There was far too great a gulf between the person I was and the person I wanted to be. I was in a marriage that was a sham, in a country where I didn't feel at home, en route to another and more difficult land, moving in completely the wrong direction; I wanted to go home. Home to what? Home where? Where would we live, how would we live, we couldn't live together, that much was obvious, but we had a child, a daughter whom I loved; I had to stick to my marriage, I had to be false.

I had to be false, I was false, and I wasn't able to write; I was no longer an author.

So what was I? And what work should I do? I sat in the hotel room and drank wine and smoked cigarettes. I sat immobile at my writing table and looked at the white roses, the white lilies, the white sheets of paper; I needed something black, something dark, I had to do something bad.

After two months in Antigua we were flown from Guatemala to Nicaragua. We were to spend a month in the Norwegian Embassy's precincts in Managua. It was a large detached house surrounded by high walls topped with barbed wire and shards of broken glass. A guard at the gate, armed with a machine gun. We were shielded from the poverty and the heat, the almost unbearable heat of Managua which was interrupted by the ice-cold air conditioning in the house. The villa was so large that I can hardly recall anything about it. We inhabited a kind of prison, a cool and comfortable prison in the middle of that hard, hot city. We were two families and two single people, a socialist from the previous contingent who had left his wife and children for a young Nicaraguan girl, with whom he'd set up house in a place he'd bought outside Managua; in so doing he'd broken two of Norad's key rules: it was forbidden to buy property in Nicaragua, and you were supposed to keep your hands off the Nicaraguan women. The other Peace Corps worker in the house was Johan Brox. He wrote articles for Norad's house magazine, one of them was entitled 'Johan Lackland', and another 'Don Johan in Nicaragua', it described the difficulties of saying no to all the girls who offered their services in the house where he lived alone.

We sat on the terrace of the indoor garden in the evenings, drinking rum and discussing conditions in Nicaragua. On Revolution Day, the nineteenth of July, I drove off to hear Daniel Ortega's speech; he stood on a colossal stage surrounded by scantily clad girls who danced as he spoke, dancing to hold the audience's attention; Ortega spoke for three hours without a break.

When at last he'd finished, his listeners ran riot. They overturned cars, poured petrol on tyres, set fire to the rubber and tipped red dye into the fountain in the Plaza de la Republica. They set off rockets and hurled bangers into the crowds. I jogged back to the car, we'd been given our own car by Norad, a red Toyota pickup. The vehicle had a flatbed for cargo, and this was crowded with small boys who were looking after the car while I was away. If I didn't pay them, they would scratch the car's paint with their knives. I paid what they demanded and drove out of the city centre. Each time I stopped at a red light, several things would happen simultaneously: two boys would leap on to the bonnet and begin washing the windscreen. The water was so dirty that it was almost impossible to see through the windscreen when the washing was finished. I lowered my window and paid for the work. At the same moment, a man would come over and stick a handful of cigarette packets into the car's interior. Reluctantly, I bought two packets of Marlboro. The man was immediately super-seded by two young girls in white shorts and tight, white tee shirts; they wanted to get into the car, to give it a blow job, as they put it, it would cost such-and-such number of dollars. While this was going on, the bed of the pickup would fill with men and women. They didn't do anything, didn't want anything, just sat on the back of the pickup for the ride through the city, until the next time I hit a red light. Then they jumped down. More got on. The windscreen was washed yet again, people hawked cigarettes and handkerchiefs, other small girls with tight pants and unbuttoned shirts knotted over their stomachs and under their breasts, bent in at the driver's window. I realized from all this that I'd better stop driving through town. Walking had to be preferable. But it wasn't. As a young man with fair skin, it was impossible to wander free and unmolested here. Even with a hat and dark glasses, unshaven and wearing old, dark clothes, it was impossible to walk at will through the streets of Managua. It just wasn't feasible, and after a few days I gave up any attempt at walking about the town; I kept to the house, with my family, we bought our supplies, and ate out, in the vicinity of the house, in the embassy district.

*

Then the day arrived for moving to our own house in the mountains.

We loaded the little we owned onto the Toyota and drove in a small Norad convoy towards Matagalpa. Gradually, the road got narrower and more potholed; it was as if we were driving in the last days, towards some final destination, it would be difficult to return.

Agnete drove, technically the car belonged to her. It would be used for work, by the theatre group, they were to travel around the mountains and villages, do theatre; I was to stay at home with the child.

Our daughter was now two years old; she was moved around, following us as a child must follow its parents.

I really hope she's forgotten that journey, those years, that she doesn't remember anything of her childhood.

She was often ill, didn't like the heat, got temperatures, lay sleepless and hot at night. She threw up and cried, she struggled with all the changes, all the uncertainties, with the sweltering days and the sun, the nights and the insects, the dogs that howled, the sounds and the smells, with Guatemala and Nicaragua, with parents who barely spoke to each other.

This silence between her parents must have had its effect on her.

The silence was there in the car, between us, like a heavy, hot cloud; we said almost nothing all of that long journey from Managua to our house in Matagalpa.

And when we saw the house, our new home, we began to argue.

I thought the house was too big, the surrounding area was poor.

It was practically a villa, two-storeyed, with a garage, surrounded by the familiar security wall; a new prison, but this time it was our home.

This genteel house stood on a dirt street of shacks and clusters of run-down little houses, it was a poor street.

Agnete was enchanted. The house was large and beautiful. Big rooms, an open, modern kitchen; just through the front door on the left, a round kitchen table and a window with a view of the mountains that encircled the town: It's almost like being back home, she said.

A dining room on the right, three steps up to a large, open living room; what were we going to do with it, with all this space? Three bedrooms, a bathroom. More stairs, to the floor above, three more rooms, one of them with a view of the mountains, that could be my workroom.

We argued about the house.

I didn't like it, I wasn't used to living like a rich man with my own garage and car, a detached house in the heart of a poor district. Agnete loved large houses, luxury, wealth. I said: We should have asked for a smaller house. I was the one who'd be at home, with the child, I was the one who'd have to try to maintain normal relations with our neighbours.

The first night we spent in it the house was completely empty, no furniture, no life, the three of us slept in the biggest bedroom, frightened of the dark, all the noises, the dogs that barked, that howled at the night. We had to lock a special metal gate in front of the door, then we locked the door and all the windows were protected with metal grilles which we secured one after the other.

We locked the empty house. We lay awake in the same bedroom. Agnete and Amalie shared the double bed, I lay in another bed covered with a mosquito net, as I'd said no to malaria tablets. I lay awake all night long listening to the mosquitoes whining in the bedroom, were they outside or inside the mosquito net? I lay staring into the dark. The room was intensely hot. We had no air conditioning, the bedroom window couldn't be opened; it was a night out of hell.

In the early hours I saw two human shapes in the bedroom. A young girl and an elderly man, they were wearing masks, black fabric masks over their eyes; were they returning from a party? Was it a break-in? A dream? I sat up in bed and shouted. The forms shrank slowly back, clasping one another, as if they'd been discovered doing something intimate, something criminal, the old man and the young girl, they vanished through the door, I sat in bed pointing: Did you see them? I asked Agnete.

The very next morning the actors arrived. They resembled soldiers, six young girls in uniform, military trousers and boots, black tee shirts; they called themselves Sandinistas. The women sat in the kitchen and held a conference. They found it strange that the house was so big, and amusing that Agnete had a husband who was going to stay at home with the baby. He's an author, Agnete said. She liked saying she was married to an author, but the author hadn't written a single word since he'd married her, that was the reality. The actors ended their meeting and saluted before driving off with Agnete to a venue somewhere in the mountains.

I was alone in the house with my daughter.

There was a knock at the door. It was the first of many women who came to the house asking for water. It seemed we had a well in the garden, and that this well was the only one in the neighbourhood with any water in it. It lasted a few days and then the well ran dry. I let the woman in, she went out to the kitchen, filled two plastic cans with water, thanked me and left. It was only a few minutes before another woman with plastic containers knocked at the door. I let her in. One of the women asked if I needed help in the house, she could clean and cook. She could look after my little girl, do the shopping and wash my clothes. I said I had a wife and that I wanted to be alone in the house. But where is this wife of yours? She's working, I said. But why are you alone in the house with the little girl? they asked. And that's how it went on, day after day; I realized the best thing was to vacate the house, for a few hours in the middle of the day; and that's how it was that my daughter and I came to take the dirt road down the hill towards Matagalpa town centre.

It was soon brought home to me that for a man in the prime of life, it was practically a disgrace to have only one child. And the word went around that this man spent all his time at home alone looking after his child. Each day the man and the child took a walk into town, what did they do there?

There wasn't a lot to do in Matagalpa. Most of the time was spent fending people off: men who wanted to change money, who wanted to buy dollars, who wanted to sell cigarettes, women who wanted to sell themselves. We went to the market to buy vegetables. I bought flowers and eggs, butter and meat; we walked among the stalls where animal carcases and sausages hung, where there were displays of fresh foods and cheese, milk and bread. I bought new clothes for Amalie, clothes that would make her look like other children in Matagalpa. But the new clothes had the opposite effect, people pointed and laughed, she stuck out, her fair skin red and sunburnt. Her long, fair hair which people often ran their fingers through; she kept close to me when we walked through town. I decided to travel home. Not tomorrow, not next week, but one day, before our two years in Matagalpa were up, I'd travel home with my daughter.

Late in the afternoon, after work, before it was dark, Agnete and I would go out buying furniture for the house. We bought a hammock, a rocking chair, a low, cedarwood coffee table. It would take us a long time to furnish the big house, before the house would seem at all normal, like a house, an inhabitable dwelling. In the evenings, darkness fell early, we had to lock the iron gate and the door behind it, close the windows and secure the window grilles. We'd been warned not to leave anything lying around outside, gardening tools, garden furniture, bicycles, games, anything, because they'd get stolen. We sat in the empty living room waiting for it to be bedtime, so that we could turn in. I'd stay up for a while in the living room to listen to the radio, to write a bit, I said; I'd begun to drink a little in the evenings. It was alcohol that finally enabled me to relax, to be myself, for a few hours, it was alcohol that helped me sleep at night, that prevented me from becoming ill, it was alcohol, I believed, that kept me healthy. I had a small collection of bottles hidden away in my workroom, and one evening all the bottles were gone, every one of them. Was this the evening to tell her I was leaving? No, my plan wasn't yet ripe, it hadn't been worked out well enough, I had to be patient, not get excited, I had to wait.

One day the phone rang, it was Jan, the father of the other Peace Corps family, they lived in a village in the mountains; the family was lying flat on the floor when he rang, we could hear the machine-gun salvos down the phone. It's the peasants raiding the local bank, he told us. It's not the first time, when the peasants have no food or money, when they're sufficiently hungry and desperate, they raid the banks. Tomorrow, Jan said, Ortega will send in his soldiers to put down the rebellion, as he calls it, then there'll be more shooting. The following day, I was sitting in the garden reading, Amalie playing in the shade of the garden trees, as the lorries of soldiers arrived. Three lorries with young boys on the back, nineteen- or twenty-year-old youths with machine guns in their laps, they sat on the backs of the lorries smoking cigarettes. The trucks rolled past the house, only a few yards from the garden; for an instant I exchanged a look with one of the boys, and in that moment I was terrified the vehicle would stop and the soldiers would ransack the house, take what they wanted, that hard, covetous look, it left me utterly defenceless, and it was in that moment I made up my mind to go.

There were stirrings of civil war in Nicaragua. But the disturbances throughout the country were overshadowed by the war that raged in our house. There was war in the house and in the country; we listened to the news on the radio, we heard gunfire in the mountains, but the bursts of fire were drowned out by screams and shouts, by slamming doors, breaking bottles and splintering furniture.

The house was destroyed from within and without.

Perhaps it would have been better if the house had been threatened from the outside.

We fastened the door and the gate from the inside, shut the windows and locked the grilles, we shut ourselves inside the house; now we were safe; now we could go for each other.

We could destroy the house, the home, the family, each other, our marriage, everything.

It was a liberation.

*

We'd been told that if the unrest in Matagalpa increased, we were to phone the embassy, and we'd be evacuated or moved back to Managua. In the end we rang and asked to be helped to leave the house in Matagalpa. The embassy sent a car, and while we waited for it, I packed the Toyota with my most important possessions: my typewriter, some books and clothes; that was all I had of importance. I also packed some of Amalie's toys and clothes; she was going home with me, that was the plan; if Agnete wanted to remain in Nicaragua, that was her choice.

I'd saved money for the journey home. The most difficult thing, I discovered, was that the banks only paid out local currency, and the airline would accept nothing but US dollars. It would cost almost 5,000 dollars to send my family and our luggage home. Where would I get hold of these American dollars? The bank clerk in Matagalpa told me there were illegal bureaux de change in Managua where I could buy dollars. But it was expensive and not without risk. I'd have to be wary and vigilant, count and check all the notes, they were often counterfeit.

Five thousand dollars.

Most likely it would be paid out in hundred-dollar bills; I'd have to count them, then I'd have to walk with the money through Managua, from the bureau de change to the airline headquarters where I'd pay with the notes which, hopefully, would be genuine.

Even this wouldn't be the hardest bit. The hardest thing would be to take my daughter home with me. Agnete insisted on remaining in Nicaragua, completing her work in Matagalpa. She wanted to live in the house with Amalie. She'd employ a nanny, she said.

I was playing for high stakes.

I was almost sure Agnete wouldn't stay in Nicaragua if I went home.

It would have been madness.

But neither of us was normal, we were both short of energy and common sense. The sense had been sucked out of us by the heat and the passion, by the dark, long nights and intense days in the locked and isolated house in Matagalpa.

We left the house.

I would willingly have set fire to it, watched it burn to the ground.

I was in a good spirits.

We were driving away from Matagalpa on the bumpy, cratered road, it was a good road, it was going in the right direction. I was on my way home.

A few days later I sat in the back of a taxi perspiring, full of anxiety; it was extremely hot, I had a small pack on my back full of Nicaraguan cordobas, enough money to keep my taxi driver in funds for several years, the sun was scorching, I was entirely at the mercy of this cabbie's goodwill. I studied him in the mirror, was he a good person, what does a good person look like; I want to buy some American dollars, I said, take me to the most businesslike bureau de change. Where would he take me? He drove slowly, that was unusual, he lit a cigarette, a Mercedes automatic, old; we floated through Managua. We were floating on a wave of heat, the sultry air lay like a thin, quivering liquid on the windscreen, we drove further and further into the city.

We sank into the city.

Deeper and deeper down to the bottom of the city.

Now where were we?

The car stopped in a wide street; a special stillness filled it, as when sharks have chased the small fish away, still, dangerous water. A quiet street on the edge of town; I was in the middle of a bad film, but I was beginning to get used to this film, it had been running for some months now; it was just a case of behaving like an idiot, and the film would run on, and everything would be all right, or would it?

We drew up in front of a brick building, several storeys, no sign, but there was a guard at the main entrance. He was unarmed, that was a bad sign. It meant he was guarding an illicit business, and that the weapons were inside.

I'll wait here, said my driver.

That won't be necessary, I replied, and paid what he asked for the trip and the service, and hoped he'd be gone when I emerged from the bureau.

I got out of the taxi, approached the guard and said I wanted to buy dollars. How many? he asked. I told him. He checked me for weapons, tapped a code into the door lock. Then he led me into a narrow hall-way, opened a door on the right and we went in.

A short thickset man in uniform sat behind a desk. Next to the desk stood a man in a similar uniform with a machine gun. Were they soldiers? It wasn't unusual for soldiers in Ortega's Sandinista army to have their sidelines: assassinations, extortion, prostitution, nar-cotics, currency exchange. I seated myself in a leather armchair. Would I like a cigarette? Yes, please. A glass of rum? Yes. They wanted to see my passport. What was I doing in Nicaragua? I told them. What was I going to do with the money? Buy airline tickets and send some luggage; I wanted to go home. What sum in dollars? I was asked to write the amount on a piece of paper. Then the man behind the desk began tapping on a calculator. He held the calculator out and showed me the total I had to pay in cordobas. I opened my backpack, counted out the money. He checked the amount, got up and went out of a door behind the desk. I sat there looking at the man with the gun. He appeared relaxed, friendly. He poured more rum into my glass. It made me feel better. The squat soldier returned with the dollar bills in wads. He counted out the money, snapped the elastic bands around the notes and handed them to me, giving me a look which I've only seen once before, and the effect now was the same as it had been then—it froze my blood. I was frightened. I didn't dare remove the bands and count the money. I put the money into my pack, got up and held out my hand. He didn't take it, only gestured towards the door. I was accompanied out by the guard who'd entered the office with me. This was the most dangerous bit. Would he follow me and steal back the money in another street? This was something I'd thought about, the people at the bureau de change and the taxi driver who drove me there figured in my risk-assessment, as well as the usual dangers of walking through Managua. I remained standing for a while on the pavement outside the main door, close to the guard, and lit a cigarette. It was a case of doing the opposite of what was expected; I wanted to appear leisurely, unhurried, I wanted to seem assured. Could I be waiting for someone? I looked at my watch, took out my mobile phone, dialled a number and spoke into it. Then I began to walk.

On a Friday in November all three of us took a plane from Managua to Miami. From there we were to fly to Madrid, then get a plane to Fornebu, where we'd spend the night at a hotel near the airport. The day after we were to fly to Bergen. When the plane from Madrid landed at Fornebu and we emerged from the plane, I began to cry. It was the cold, clear air.

The cold, ice-blue air. I inhaled deep lungfuls of it, I'd never known a better, stronger air. The air had a tiny bit of moisture in it, rain was coming. Soon it would start snowing. A thick, white snow. It would settle in the streets. It would be December, it would be Christmas. I'd got together with Agnete at Christmas, six years earlier. Now we celebrated Christmas Eve together, with my parents in Øyjordsveien. Her parents and mine, my sister and her family, Agnete's brother and his wife, Agnete and me and our daughter, we were one big family on Christmas Eve. We sat around the long table that was laid in the living room, ate and drank, my father made a speech, it was a beautiful evening, and when we parted from one another that evening the whole of our extended family dissolved.

WORKROOMS, LABORATORIES

I needed money, I had nowhere to live. My father got me a job at the factory; I was to be a kind of handyman. I painted walls, enamelled rusty pipes, cleaned and oiled the looms. I was in luck, there was a vacant flat in the caretaker's quarters which was within the factory compound. I could live there. On the first floor; two rooms, a bathroom and kitchen, from the kitchen I could look straight into the production hall where I'd be working.

Below me lived one of the women who'd been employed at the factory, on the looms in the textile mill. She was a pensioner and lived alone on the ground floor. One day when she was out doing her shopping, her flat was broken into. I came home from work and saw that her door had been smashed in; I knocked on the doorframe and she emerged, in tears, and drew me into the living room which had been completely wrecked.

A wrecked living room. It was one of the worst things I've ever seen. Someone had slashed all the sofa cushions with a knife. The same with the chairs, their upholstery had been slit. The standard lamps had been knocked over and their stands smashed. The display-unit drawers had been pulled out, their contents tipped on the floor. The china, glasses, cups, lay smashed on the ground. Her photographs had been torn from the walls or swept off the shelves. The books were strewn all over the room. A similar story in the kitchen, the contents of the cupboards and drawers had been thrown on to the floor. The same in the bedroom, wardrobes emptied and kicked to bits. The mattress had been ripped open, the duvet and pillows cut to shreds. They'd been searching for cash and pills. The bathroom had been pulled apart and smashed, the house-breaking junkies had run amok. They'd destroyed her home.

I never managed to furnish my flat. I was too tired after work, worn down and tired; I slept on a mattress in the corner of the room. Slept and worked. I fetched my daughter at the weekends, and we usually went to my parents in Øyjordsveien, I couldn't show her where and how I lived.

I'd returned to my beginnings, where my roots were: Øyjordsveien and the factory.

I worked. Got up at seven and was at my job by half past, worked till three-thirty.

It was dark when I began work, and semi-dark outside when work finished.

Agnete borrowed money from the bank and her parents, she bought an old house on the island of Askøy. It was a large property; now that she was a landowner, as she labelled herself, she wanted to establish a garden, grow vegetables, get some chickens, she wanted to go back to nature.

She was pregnant by a new boyfriend. She refurbished the old house single-handed. Put a new wooden floor in the living room. She insulated the walls, replaced panes in the windows, sanded and varnished the floors upstairs. She and her brother made a large, new kitchen counter, knocked down the dividing wall between the kitchen and the living room and opened up the poky house. With her boyfriend she built a soapstone fire-surround in the living room and a brick chimney through the roof. The house was painted white. Rose bushes were planted in front of the house, by the sunny wall outside the workroom which one day would become mine.

Agnete didn't know it, but she had only a few years left to live.

She planted roses and tulips, dug out her kitchen garden behind the house. She pruned the rhododendron bushes, lopped withered branches from the lovely apple tree which stood in the middle of the garden, right in front of the living-room window.

Soon the tree would put out small, white flowers.

Soon she would give birth to her second daughter, in May; she wanted it to be a home delivery.

It was only a few months after the birth that she split up with her new boyfriend; Agnete lived alone with two girls in the house on Askøy. It must have been a hard and difficult life, especially during the winters, it couldn't have been easy; I know this, because I was the one who ended up with the house and both the girls.

The year that her younger daughter turned three in May, Agnete died in September. She died in the house. She wanted to die at home. She'd given birth to both her daughters at home, now she wanted to die in the same way, in her own bed.

It was natural.

My mother died first, then Agnete the following year. Not long after, Agnete's father died, and then Agnete's brother; it was as if death had begun a chain reaction in the family, one misfortune following another, as when natural forces strike cities taking houses and cars, people and animals in great floods or tornadoes; for a time, I was seriously worried that I wouldn't survive this family catastrophe.

What was I to do?

Peter Handke tells of a man who was hit by a car. He was thrown into the air and landed on his feet behind the car, before continuing on his way.

TOMAS ESPEDAL

We continue on our way. As if nothing has happened? No, something has happened, something has hurt us, but we continue as if nothing has occurred.

There wasn't a lot else I could do, we had to continue as if everything was normal. I sent the girls off to school as usual, we had dinner as we'd always done, but nothing was normal.

Is calamity as prerequisite for happiness?

No, happiness arrives suddenly and unexpectedly as a totally absolute and independent quantity, it is born of the moment, like a natural event, a rainbow, a shooting star, a lightning strike or a fire, awe-inspiring and lovely; and happiness, too, changes everything.

After six years in the house on Askøy we moved to the terraced house in Øyjordsveien.

A Little Book about Happiness

For a long time I dreamt of writing a series of little books. A little book about love. A little book about friendship. A little book about writing. A little book for my daughter. A little book about happiness, et cetera.

The book about happiness could never be a long one, anyway.

Not a long book, nor yet a profound book, the language of happiness is straightforward and banal, there is no depth to happiness, or is there?

The book about happiness must be brief. Brief and fragmentary; it is impossible to create a continuous narrative about happiness. No chronology. No logic or sense; it's impossible to write a novel about happiness.

I've always been happiest indoors, rarely outside, apart from a few lightning-like flashes that illuminated something incomprehensible and new, something I'd never seen before, something in nature.

I've never had a relationship with nature. The first animal I ever saw was, I suspect, a tortoise, which our neighbours, in the flat below us, on the ninth floor, had in the living room; it mostly lived inside a box, or crawled across the lino to lie just on the edge of the carpet, drawn into its shell, which, I remember, had a beautiful pattern.

Animals weren't allowed in the flats in Skytterveien, but I gradually discovered guinea pigs and canaries, parrots and rabbits, dogs and cats, living in the blocks, probably other animals as well, small animals that were never let out.

Some of the boys had pigeon coops which they'd nailed together in the woods behind the blocks; I never saw any of the pigeons, or I didn't notice them, until word went around the street that a cat had been in one of the coops. The cat had torn the pigeons to bits, and the Saars brothers, who owned this coop, avenged themselves on the unidentified perpetrator by nailing a random cat to a tree.

From then on I noticed the pigeons; they sailed in great swoops over the buildings, a flock of grey-white birds that flew in and out of the coops on the edge of the woods. They shot out of the coops in arrow formation, describing arcs and streaks in the air, before making a neat turn towards home; I just wanted them to fly straight on and leave the coops for ever.

All of a sudden, or so it seemed, it was decided we were moving. We moved a few hundred yards, from Skytterveien to a terraced house in Øyjordsveien; there was a small garden, hardly more than a patch of earth in front of the house, about six yards by six. In the spring this little space was covered in flowers; it was a pale mauve flower with a yellow eye which grew in profusion in front of our house. I didn't know the name of the flower or what they meant to my mother but while the flowers stood thickly outside our living-room window, she prohibited all games in the garden, and my father wasn't allowed to mow the lawn before the flowers had disappeared of their own accord. It was from him I learnt that the flowers were called: your mother's cress.

With the spring, crocuses and daffodils appeared in the garden, but the first snowdrops, they were almost impossible to see, they hid beneath the bushes right next to the fence. Then the crocuses, and later the yellow lilies which my mother cut with a knife and placed in a high-necked, green vase on the living-room table. I never managed to associate these flowers with a time of year, with the transition from winter to spring; I associated them with my mother.

My mother was scared of dogs. She was scared of cats, didn't like birds, she was frightened of almost everything that moved; it always amazed me that she was never frightened of either my father or me; I was sixteen and could have knocked her down just like that, and yet she would go for us both, she'd hurl herself at me without a trace of anxiety or fear.

Every Friday my mother would buy tulips. Usually red, sometimes white, approaching Easter the flowers would be yellow, and in the summer she bought chrysanthemums or gladioli; there were always vases of flowers on the tables in the living room. There were flowers on the low bookcase that she'd inherited from her father. The books stood just as he'd arranged them in Torgallmenningen: atlases and encyclopaedias and all kinds of reference works, on birds and trees, gardens and flora, *The Plants of Norway* in two volumes by Knut Fægri, as well as collected editions of Undset's novels and Hamsun's novels, Falkberget and Duun, Collett and Lie, Skram and Bjørnson; above the books was a little collection of orchids. They were lined up at right-angles to the sun so that it lit the flowers from the side; I thought the flowers looked like butterflies, and, when the warmth of the sun touched the thin petals, they flickered like wings; it wasn't hard to imagine the flowers wanting to fly out of the little living room.

Perhaps the greatest happiness is when something remains unchanged; the house in Øyjordsveien is exactly as it was when I lived here with my parents. I haven't altered anything in the house. The living-room walls are the same colour, slightly faded, an ice-blue, cold colour which was good to sit in when the sun shone through the large windows giving on to the garden. The chairs are the same, they stand in their appointed places. The bookcase is just as it was when my mother was alive. The books are as my grandfather arranged them, that must be more than fifty years ago, before I was born, perhaps they'll be standing on the shelf like that after I'm dead; I want my daughter to have the house and the books. Maybe it won't stay like that, maybe she'll change everything, it's only natural.

Outside, everything is in flux, but inside we can keep things as they've been; the furniture, the lamps, the rooms.

Inside we can hold on to time, or cling to it; inside we're happy still, and ageless.

The living room in Øyjordsveien is unchanged. I buy the same flowers as my mother did, set them in their allotted places; there are rings from the vases on the bookcase and coffee table.

The kitchen is as it always was, deep red tiles and a cooker of the same colour. Pine kitchen cupboards, glasses and crockery that were my maternal grandmother's. The only changes are on the first floor, my boyhood bedroom has been painted pink, and there's a chandelier of plastic pearls hanging from the ceiling. This was my daughter's room. My sister's room is painted yellow, it was Janne's workroom; this was where she wrote during the years we lived together. All three of us on the cramped top floor, like a nest in the top of a tree, a small family, so close, so secure, I thought about it often as I lay next to Janne in bed and waited for us to fall asleep. The wind buffeted the bedroom window. Then the rain came on, it whipped and beat against the pane. We fell asleep together. It's a miracle, a great joy, the way two people who love each other fall asleep at the same moment.

We met at a party. It was one New Year's Eve. The language of happiness is so thoroughly simple and brutal—she was the most beautiful girl I'd ever seen.

The language of happiness can be uncomfortable— she saw me as an older man.

Or—we recognized each other immediately.

The young girl and the older man. We needed each other.

We would love each other.

How to write about happiness? What can I write about happiness when it's so simple and mundane, so quiet and transparent, as when she'd lie on the sofa and I barely saw her because I was so used to her lying on the sofa resting.

Every day she'd lie on the sofa and read.

Didn't I see her? Didn't I hear her, how she turned the pages of the book, how she breathed as she read, as if she was reading with her breath, this rhythm of respiration that must have followed the rise and fall of the sentences, the full stop, comma, question mark? What was she reading? Wasn't I concerned about it, what she read, how her breath filled the living room with happiness?

I've never been so happy in all my life.

It was only when she no longer reclined on the sofa, when she'd moved out, and our relationship was over, it was only when she'd gone and the sofa stood there big and empty in the corner of the living room, that I realized how happy I'd been.

I know now that happiness is hard to describe; it has its own quiet, invisible existence there in the daily lives of the two lovers. She lay on the sofa and rested. I was in the kitchen cooking, shouted to her that dinner was ready. Didn't I understand the happiness of her lying on the sofa reading? That we'd have dinner together? I didn't consider it; I was happy.

Ah, happy, so happy.

Year after year, three, four years, five, six, the happiness continued, it grew, year after year; I'd never have thought it possible.

I'd imagined that happiness would diminish, that it would vanish, that it would mutate into dullness and predictability, rows and irritations, that it would be consumed by daily life and triviality, but it was the opposite; happiness enveloped everything it met and grew like some great feline, it grew and grew—how would it end?

I almost wish I'd stopped loving her.

But I became more and more fond of her the longer we were together.

I wanted to be with her all the time, for ever.

So, what should I say about happiness? That I was happy as soon as I saw her when we woke up in the mornings? That I spent the whole day looking forward to the time when we went to bed together at night? We lay side by side and read. We read our separate copies of the Knausgaard books, began at the same time and read in tandem, suddenly she'd put down her book and look at me: Did you read that? she'd ask. How does he dare, it's quite extraordinary, he must have a screw loose, she'd say.

Then we read on.

Until I put down my book and looked at her; Did you read that? I'd ask. How does he dare, it's quite amazing, he's destroying himself, I'd say.

There is almost nothing to say about happiness. It's there in everything we see and do, and we don't even know about it.

Just listening to her voice. That husky, deep voice, as if her voice was older than she was, an old voice, where did it come from, where does the voice come from?

I loved hearing her speak.

And when she laughed, I began to cry.

Why are you crying? she asked, in astonishment, the first time. It's your laugh, I said. I've never heard anything like it. How so? Your laughter isn't like you. Who's it like then? Like someone you'll turn into one day, I said. Oh, Tomas, she said, I'm not going to leave you. I love you.

I love you too.

I loved absolutely everything about her. Her hands, her mouth, her hair, her back, everything. And the things she wore and the things she owned. There was nothing I didn't like about her. Nothing. There was nothing that irritated me apart, perhaps, from the length of time she took in the shower—she could spend a very long time under hot water.

I told her about the time I'd stayed at a hotel on the edge of the Sahara; there was a notice on the bathroom door that explained, in English, that this was a desert and that we had to save water. Each morning an American girl showered away our entire allowance of washing water. I used some unkind epithets about Americans, but Janne didn't like this story, she interrupted me halfway through: Yeah, yeah, she said, but we live in Bergen and I'm tired of hearing about all your travels.

Was that the first sign? The first sign of discontent in her? I was older than her, and she missed Oslo.

Could I live with her in Oslo? Could we transfer our happiness there?

We'd gone to dinner with friends; they'd just bought a flat on the east side of Oslo, at Torshov. She was a writer and he a painter; I bought two pornographic pictures from him, the pictures had been shown at the Autumn Exhibition. (When Pushwagner had seen them, he'd executed a pirouette in front of them, it was clearly a sign that he approved of something; he did his pirouette and moved on.) We cemented the deal with champagne and, as we raised our glasses on the balcony, and stood looking out over huge brick buildings, Janne suddenly chimed in, loudly, I could never live on the east side.

I laughed all evening at this outburst. I was still laughing as we sat in the taxi going home to her parents at Østerås. I could never live on the east side, I repeated, again and again; I put my arms around Janne and kissed her ceaselessly on the cheek and the hair and the mouth. I didn't perceive the seriousness of her comment. But it's true, she said. I don't want to look at other people's brick walls, I must have a view, she said.

From the house we shared in Bergen, we had a view of Askøy, we could even see over the island and right out to sea.

I was happy in the house with her. But it wasn't her house, her place, her city. Wasn't she as happy as I was? I don't know, but I think she was happy in the wrong place. Is the place more important than happiness? I don't know, but there must have been some disparity between us; I didn't spot it, didn't notice it, I was happy.

And there is something in happiness that settles over the eyes. A thin, undetectable film, transparent as water or glass, not unpleasant, no, a delicate veil over the eyes, it blurs the vision, dulls the sight, I didn't see her.

And there is something in happiness that settles over the body. A new skin, it grows over the old, a thin, fine, wax-like membrane that stretches and accommodates itself softly and exactly to the body; I no longer noticed how she was feeling.

And there is something in happiness that makes you forget. A sweetish, white substance that spreads around the body in the blood, it enters every organ and is pumped out into the hands and fingers, down to the legs and penis, up to the face and into the eyes, out to the ears, along the nose, into the mouth and tongue, all across the skin. There is something about happiness that makes everything novel, that makes the past disappear, you're inattentive and lose concentration; I forgot how difficult love is.

I was completely happy.

Occasionally, when she was speaking or laughing, I felt as if she was older than me.

And when I laid my face between her breasts, I was ageless.

Happiness was like a mask, it had tightened over my eyes and face like a finely woven black mask; I sat on her lap, she drew my head towards her breasts, it was as if time had been turned upside down in a terrible revolution; I became the younger one.

I was exactly twice her age.

The first time he saw us together, one of my friends said: You're identical, you're like brother and sister.

We borrowed a car and took a holiday trip to Gothenburg. Janne drove, she drove fast, we drove fast to Gothenburg. We went to an exhibition of photographs at the Art Museum, and bumped into Martin Larsson, an artist who'd lived in Bergen. We sat in the cafe with him. As we were about to leave, he stretched out a hand: It was lovely meeting you and your daughter, he said.

It was always happening. We'd go out together, and someone would come over and want to meet my daughter.

It was shameful.

We were ashamed.

Where did this sense of shame come from?

Was happiness shameful; our happiness was shameful, it wasn't natural, it went against nature.

We ceased going out, we shut ourselves indoors.

In the kitchen: she stood cutting up meat with the sharp, pointed meat knife. Pushed the tip into the meat, cut through sinew, cut away fat and bone. Wiped away the blood with a paper towel. Those large hands of hers, her hair tied in a ponytail. A red apron, a white, tight-fitting tee shirt. Blue jeans, Birkenstock sandals. A white tablecloth, grey plates, green napkins, a carafe of water, candles. We had olives and feta cheese, beef with potatoes, asparagus and butter. Another bottle of wine, we sat side by side on the kitchen unit, smoking and talking. Then I took off her jeans. Pulled off her apron. Panties, sandals. We made love. I grabbed the carafe from the table and poured water over her hair and face. Poured cold water over her tee shirt. How transparent and wet the material became. How hard her nipples got. She gasped for breath. As if she was drowning; I poured more and more water over her.

In the bedroom: she lay close by the bedside lamp reading. Sometimes in a white nightdress, sometimes in a grey one, sometimes, in the summer, with the window open, she read with no nightdress on.

In the bathroom: she stood under the shower, and the bathroom was thick with steam. I could only just make her out in all that steam, as if she'd vanished in mist, in a white winter frost, a white winter landscape, winter in the warmth; my arms reached out for her.

In the living room: white curtains moving in the breeze, the warm summer breeze. Strong sunlight, the patio door open, a bath towel on the lawn. She moved around the living room in a new swimsuit, searching for something; I lay on the sofa and thought I was the luckiest man alive.

I was happy in every room of the house.

We made love in the living room, in the kitchen, in the basement, in the bathroom, in the bedroom. On the floor, on the sofa, on the tables, on the chairs, everywhere.

Sometimes we'd open the bedroom window, she would lean out of the first-floor window; it was almost like making love outdoors.

But we stayed inside. We remained indoors.

We painted the bedroom dark brown, almost black, put up cream-coloured curtains. We finally managed to arrange our books on bookshelves, we covered the walls with books, her books and my books, we immured ourselves behind books.

We read and wrote.

When we went out, out of the house, we left singly, rarely together.

She cycled off to the university.

I walked to the shop.

We lived two separate lives outside, inside we were together the whole time.

We were happy indoors. Completely together, breathing in sympathy, almost, even when we sat in our own rooms. She sat in her workroom on the top floor, I wrote in the room in the basement. I could hear her footsteps above; when she went to the bathroom, the water gurgling in the pipes, it must have been late, near bedtime, but I sat on for a while, to postpone and tease out the joy of going up the stairs, lying down beside her in bed, to sit on for a while, smoke a last cigarette, sit a bit longer at my table and write one more sentence; I wanted to write a book about happiness.

The book about happiness: it must be short. Today I saw a wagtail on the lawn in front of the house, it's the first time for many years that I've noticed one. It's definite, spring is coming, it should be a pleasure.

And the snowdrops are coming. The crocuses are coming. The daffodils are coming. Even the cress is coming, it should be a pleasure, but all these things that are coming simply give me pain.

I live alone. Janne has moved to Oslo.

My daughter, too, has gone to Oslo; but I was prepared for that, misfortunes don't come singly.

There's nothing I can do about any of this; I must go on as if everything is normal. How is this possible? How many times will we be able to carry on, as if nothing's happened; the car is approaching, at top speed, it's the second time it hits us, we're thrown up in the air and land behind the car, but this time we just lie there. We don't get up.

Jacques Roubaud wrote that his wife's wristwatch went on ticking for a long time after she was dead.

That's just how it is; happiness has fled, but it continues to cause pain for a long time after the relationship is over.

In *The Story of My Misfortunes* Peter Abélard wrote: 'Whether awakening the human passions or trying to soothe them, the power of example is often greater than that of words, and after giving you some words of comfort, I decided to write to you where you live now, and tell you about my troubles. I hope you will realize that, compared to them, your own afflictions are as nothing, or at least extremely insignificant, and that that will make them easier to bear.'

The thirty-eight-year-old Abélard was in love with sixteen-year-old Héloïse. There are many advantages in a relationship between an older man and a younger woman. The young woman has a man with experience; no longer restless and immature, he may have accumulated some wealth, a position in society. The young woman can depend on the older man. She can rely on his desiring her. She can rely on his not being concerned with anyone apart from her. All his talents and abilities are focused on her. He spends what means he has on her. She eats well, converses well and makes love well with her older man. He worships the young woman, is completely absorbed by her, by her body, skin, throat, hair, hands. Her movements. The way she walks, talks, her youthful manner. Once admitted to the confidence of this young woman, he'll never let her go. He'll do anything for her. He'll do anything in the world to keep her.

But the difference in age, at first such a blessing, such a joy, can quickly turn to the opposite. Abélard wrote: 'What sorrow for Héloïse's uncle when he discovered our relationship. What pain for us lovers when we had to part! What shame and confusion for me! With broken heart, I wept at the agonies the young girl had to endure!'

Abélard has made Héloïse pregnant. He's married her in secret, put her in a convent. He's placed the newly born infant with his sister. Now Fulbert, Héloïse's uncle, accuses Abélard of exploiting the girl and trying to rid himself of her by putting her in a nunnery. The two men argue. Abélard raises his right hand to ward off Fulbert's blow. He turns and leaves the room, walks quickly out of the house, runs out to the stall and jumps on his horse, rides off, away from Fulbert's house. The house where he was Héloïse's tutor. The house where he seduced Héloïse. The house where they made love. The house where they were happy. Abélard rides away from the house; it's dark, it's late, faint moonlight, the smell of forest, of flowers, of summer and autumn,

he's riding away from something it's impossible to ride
away from, he can flee but not disappear; where will
he go? He rides home. Tells his servant that he isn't at
home. Abélard doesn't go to his bedroom as usual. He
hides away in a small, secluded room in the house. He
pulls a blanket over himself, douses the tallow lamps,
he wants to vanish, wants to sleep, but he lies awake,
feeling cold, sweating, suddenly he weeps, sobs, he
wants to be with Héloïse, to embrace her, he needs her
now. He hears sounds in the house. He's given orders
that the doors must be locked, that they must be kept
locked, now the servant is opening the doors, Abélard
can hear him. He hears the sound of boots, the sound
of dogs baying in the house, men and dogs; they're
searching for him. Abélard sits up in bed, he can hear
his servant outside the door. The door is thrown open,
and the room is lit up with torches. Fulbert and three
men, they release the dogs. The dogs lunge forward,
biting and ripping at the blanket with which Abélard is
covering himself. Then he's forced back and down
on to the bed. A man sits on his head. His hands are
gripped by other hands. A man straddles his legs;
Abélard is held fast. His hose is cut off. He sees the
knife and screams. Hands hold him firmly, a rag is

stuffed in his mouth. They sit on him; a man on his head, another on his chest. The man on his chest leans forwards and slices off his testicles, a quick cut. Abélard hardly feels it, he feels the warmth and the blood, the wetness between his legs. They release him and throw him some strips of cloth. He clutches the material, presses it to the wound, to his genitals, to where his genitals used to be.

Fifteen years later, Peter Abélard wrote, in what has become known as his Letter of Comfort, to a friend:

'When morning arrived, the whole town was gathered in front of my house. It would be difficult, nay, impossible to express how stunned with dismay the people were, how they wept and complained and troubled me with shouts and screams. The clerks and my students were especially irritating with their vociferous lamentations. I suffered more from their sympathy than I did from my wounds, and felt my shame more deeply than I did my disfigurement, more from that dishonourable bashfulness than from the pain.'

How, at one stroke, happiness is turned to its opposite: the deepest despair, and loneliness; Abélard shuts himself away in a monastery, the abbey of St Denis outside Paris. Only a few months previously he'd been a famous and respected author with a young lover, a happy and privileged man, doing well in life, courted, admired, now suddenly he's in the dust, stripped of everything: honour, fame, lover, child and house; he's alone.

He's back in that small room, his workroom. His writing room. Abélard furnishes the simple cell with a desk and a chair, a bed, writing materials and books. In the evenings, after his duties, after prayers, after meals, Abélard sits hunched over his desk in the light from the tallow lamp, he reads and writes. 'I admit that in this state of contrition it was the feeling of shame rather than reawakened fervour or piety that drove me to seek a hiding place in a monastery.'

Abélard writes. In a state of contrition he writes poetry and pieces of prose, notebooks and letters. In the years after the tragedy, Abélard writes as never before; it's as if sorrow and seclusion give Abélard's writing a new depth, a new power. The contrite Abélard writes his deepest and most personal works, it's in these difficult, sorrow-laden years that Abélard becomes a writer.

What would have happened if Abélard had continued happy?

We don't know, but we wouldn't have the autobiographical *The Story of My Misfortunes*. And we wouldn't have the exchange of letters between Abélard and Héloïse, the letters in which Héloïse describes how despite all the adversity, despite all the humiliation and the harshness of a nun's life at the convent of Argenteuil, despite the loss of husband and child, she has retained her love for Abélard. The first letter she writes to Abélard, more than fifteen years after their brutal separation, is prefaced with a dedication:

> To her lord or rather her father,
> to her spouse or rather her brother,
> from his handmaiden or rather his daughter,
> his wife or rather his sister Héloïse.

THE NOTEBOOKS

Monday 19 April, evening, Øyjordsveien.

So the house is empty.

The house is empty and completely still.

Not a sound from the furniture, the sofa, the reading lamp, or from the kitchen table, or from the beds in the rooms above the living room, not a sound; a dark pall descends on the sofa where she used to lie, a thin, dark pall over the sofa and the reading lamp, over the coffee table and bookshelves, the furniture becomes soft and indistinct before it disappears completely in the evening gloom.

When I've switched off all the lights, one after the other, and the rooms are in darkness, I can even imagine the house without me.

How the rooms will repose in the semi-darkness that fills the house in the evenings, every evening, but always darker, in spite of the spring, in spite of the light, darker with each person who moves out; first my lover, then my daughter, they relinquish the house to this darkness which only increases with each day they're gone.

It's not hard to imagine how I'll become swathed in darkness, as when one wraps a black ribbon round and round the figure that sits alone in the large living room; he wants to be black, he wants to disappear.

A few days ago the house still echoed with sounds and noise, the noise of someone moving, gathering up their things and pushing them out, shoving them out through the door. Today the house is still.

It's the stillness that remains after someone's left; suddenly the house is empty of their effects, the sounds cease simultaneously, and probably their smells will vanish soon, too.

The smell of her clothes. The wardrobes are empty, but they still smell of perfume, and then there's that smell that emanates from the body itself, and which clings to its clothes, and which remains in the cupboards long after the clothes have gone.

Tuesday 20 April

The smells are still here; it's like living with shadows, you recognize the smell and continue to hear the sounds their originators made, which linger after them, it's just imagination, all is silent, but you hear the sounds.

A few days ago the sounds were real. The shower water in the bathroom, it wasn't imagination. Someone was showering. It was a good and alarming sound, water running. It ran and ran. I lay in bed thinking that soon all the hot water would be gone. It irritated me, the time she could spend in the shower. Now the bathroom is silent. Yesterday I got up early and turned on the water in the shower before returning to bed where I lay and listened to the water splashing in the empty cubicle.

A thick wall of steam in the bathroom in the morning, you could almost believe it concealed a body, as if the steam was a cocoon and the body still hid somewhere in all that steam. But the bathroom was empty. Only running water and moisture; and maybe a sort of mirage of a figure with one white bath towel around its bust and waist, another around its head and long hair, just a trick of the vision, just as unreal as when, each morning, she emerged from the bathroom shrouded in those white bath towels.

And beneath the pillow: a thin, golden hair, exactly the length of her hair when she left the bed, or was it from the time I caught her by her hair? When could she have lost that hair; it causes a terrible stab, or jolt, or whatever it is that lurches through my body taking all the air within me and compressing it into a hard lump. You toss and turn in bed. It's almost impossible to describe lovesickness, but that slender hair makes the finder's heart beat so fast and hard that he's afraid of losing his breath.

Wednesday 21 April

Three peaches in a bowl, on the kitchen unit. Every morning she'd have fruit. Oranges, apples, pears, she'd cut the fruit up with a knife and eat the pieces: now there are three peaches in a bowl, she never got around to eating them. They lie there round, red and yellowish with a cleft in their skin, the cleft in the fruit that makes it impossible not to think of her back. The peaches have begun to shrivel, their skin has got softer, soon they'll start to rot; I can't bring myself to throw them out.

With each day that passes their plump forms turn more and more wrinkled, there are dark blotches of decay, as if someone's hit them or pushed a finger too hard into the silky skin. The peaches will be inedible one day, and perhaps they'll smell, perhaps they'll stink so much I'll have to throw them out.

She's everywhere in the house, everywhere she's absent.

Every day I find it strange that I don't fall, don't fall to pieces, that I manage to walk erect, that I'm able to go around the house, that in some strange way I can stand her absence.

Why don't I fall to pieces, how do I manage to stand, why don't I crawl on the floor, how can I sit, lie, walk, why don't I crawl about on all fours?

An entire day without her, a long night. Two days, three, Saturday, Sunday, Monday, an entire week, a month, the whole of April, perhaps a year; it's too much for me to think about. Occasionally I think about minutes, hours, that I won't manage an hour more without her, how will I succeed for a whole year.

I've never loved anyone like Janne. My big romance at the age of forty-eight, that's lethal.

Thursday 22 April

The house is beautiful.

It's a beautiful house.

The house is beautiful even without her. With her in it the house was good, now it's a bad and beautiful house.

The house is small, it's got three storeys. When you come through the front door, you're right in the living room, which is little. A little living room with large windows overlooking the sea. The light is never the same in the living room; there is rain light and sunlight and cloud light. The light is never the same, sometimes the light in the living room is so bright that the room seems uninhabitable.

Just a light-room for a living room.

When the living room's in darkness, it's filled with lights, with the lights from the city and the bridge, a shining chain from the city to the island of Askøy. Then there's the light from the lamps, my mother's lamps and my lamps and Janne's lamps which she left behind.

I can't explain this love of lamps, but Janne shared it, she left her lamps behind. If she'd taken a single one of them, I would have begun to argue, shout, fight, but she left them here, and I said almost nothing when she went.

Maybe the living room is uninhabitable.

There are eight lamps in the living room. I could easily have filled the living room with lamps, but it would have looked odd, as if I had a problem of some sort, it would have frightened people who came to visit, like discovering a room is full of infection, but no one comes to visit, not after she left; no one wants to visit a house which is sick of a broken heart.

I don't quite know how to be alone in the house. What do people do? What should I do with myself? Sometimes I sit in the same chair too long. Sometimes I just stand there, immobilized by nothing, that total nothing that has filled the whole house.

Often I stay in bed as long as I can. I get up reluctantly and make breakfast, it's midday or one o'clock, then I go back to bed—isn't the smell of her still clinging to the bedclothes? Sometimes I jump out of bed and sit in the wardrobe and hug one of the dresses she's left behind. Ah, how wretched you are, I say. The abandoned are simply wretched, that's all they are, simply wretched, why lie about it; I sit on the floor in the wardrobe and cry.

Friday 23 April

Suddenly I'm scared of being alone in the house. I'd never have believed it, a week ago I'd have considered a little solitude a good thing; maybe my daughter visiting her boyfriend, maybe my girlfriend going out with some of her friends, it would mean an evening alone in the house; I looked forward to it.

Alone in the house now, I sit completely immobile in the living room talking to myself, or to the woman who isn't there; she's my only company.

What is it I'm afraid of?

I'm afraid of being alone.

It was difficult when Agnete died and I was left alone with Harriet and Amalie in the house on Askøy. But this is difficult in a more dangerous way; now I'm alone with myself.

Ole Robert's wife, Marit, says: He likes being alone as long as I'm at home.

A long, loving relationship is contained in this simple statement, a quite special beauty in this assertion, a long love story lies at the bottom of this everyday situation: he likes being alone as long as she's at home.

My situation is the worst imaginable; I love her and she isn't there.

Saturday 24 April

Why not travel, to where? She's gone away everywhere, it won't help travelling to somewhere else where she isn't, it'll make it all worse; I'd be alone in a place she'd never been to.

And if she has been there, if we've been there together, I couldn't bear it; I'd break down in Dubrovnik, or in Istanbul.

Narve drops in unexpectedly, he's driven from Førde. We sit in the kitchen as usual, smoke cigarettes and drink as usual. Nothing is normal. He's wearing his usual white shirt. His dark, shoulder-length hair covers his face when he laughs. As always he rests his left hand on the table, the hand with its stiff, stunted finger, it's got a life of its own, this finger, well, the whole hand has; It's not under my control, he says. Janne's moved to Oslo, I tell him. And Amalie is with her boyfriend, she wants to move to Oslo, too. Why don't you move to Oslo? he asks, and that sets us off laughing, and we can't stop. Why don't you move to Oslo? he says again with sudden seriousness, he pulls back his hand, rests it in his lap, watches me sternly as I laugh so much the tears run down my face.

Sunday 25 April

I'm a person who's been abandoned. That means I'm a person who remains; I can't do anything else, I can't do anything but remain in the house I live in.

It's a beautiful, quiet house, perhaps it's uninhabitable?

On the first floor there's a bathroom, next door to my daughter's room which is painted pink, the bathroom is situated between her room and Janne's workroom which is painted yellow; from this room a door leads into our bedroom, we painted that a dark brown colour, I think all the rooms are beautiful, and all the rooms are empty.

I sleep and write in the basement. The basement has a living room which I've fitted up as a workroom. I sit eight feet below ground and write. Here I work undisturbed, without disturbing anyone. Occasionally I forget there's no longer anyone to disturb, that it makes no difference if I smoke or play loud music while I'm writing. No one will hear me, no one will notice the smell of my cigarettes, no one will read my diaries and notebooks; I could move up to the living room or to one of the rooms on the top floor, but I stay in the basement, it's the only room in the house where everything is normal.

Monday 26 April

Nothing is normal, not even in the basement. It's not the same, sitting down there knowing someone is in the house as sitting down there knowing no one's in the house. The difference is so immense that it's hard to describe; I might be sitting in the basement trying to write about being alone, and suddenly it strikes me that no one's in the house, it's as if lightning has blown the main fuse: the typewriter stops, total darkness fills the basement.

Tuesday 27 April

One day so young, the next old, so young, so old that the sudden transition bowls you over, it gathers up all the years into one hard blow: age hits you in the face like a little girl.

The six-year-old from next door, Ulrikke, asks, as I open the front door a crack before hurrying out with the rubbish, I can't see her, she's standing in her Wendy house in the communal garden, but I hear her voice coming out of the little house: Where is Janne?

What am I to say?

I haven't told anyone that Janne's left, as if to postpone the dreadful news that she's gone, as if to preserve her a little longer in the house, a shade that's now being probed by the light from the keen little voice: Where is Janne? What am I to say? For a moment I'm tempted into a dangerous game: Isn't she in the Wendy house with you? Perhaps she's hiding behind the house as usual, down by the hedge, or behind that tree, she'll turn up soon, she'll get tired of hiding, she'll be back soon, you'll see.

Wednesday 28 April

Come back to me.

Come back to me.

Oh, baby, please come back to me, goes Nick Cave's 'Love Letter'. Can I write the same to her, can I ask her to please come back, baby? She loved listening to Nick Cave, but she'd hate hearing his words from me. If I implored her to return, I'd lose her for good. Maybe it would be better to write:

I'm doing fine now

I'm doing fine now

Oh, baby, I won't be missing you.

Love letter: isn't it better to lie? If I put down the truth—that I can't manage without you, that I'll fall apart without you, that I think I'll die without you, I depend on you for everything, I need you, I love you, you must help me, save me. Come back, come back to me, please, or it'll be all over with me, if I wrote the truth, she'd be livid, filled with contempt, I'd lose her for good.

Love letter: All going swingingly here. The days just seem to fly past. I'm always doing something with friends. Eating out at restaurants, drinking in my old haunts, doing all the things I didn't get the chance to do when I was with you. I've found my old self again, my old, untamed self. The money's pouring in, I'm off to Berlin in a few days' time.

Monday 3 May
Every day's a holiday.

Every day's a working day.

I think of my work as my trade. I've written every day for more than twenty years; if, because I can't be bothered, or can't manage, or for any other reason, I can't work on the novel I'm writing at the moment, I add to my notebooks, page after page in the notebooks which are my other occupation.

I've written eleven novels. And I've filled more than forty exercise books with notes; I regard them as bona-fide books.

Forty books of notes, sketches, diary entries, drawings and letters. I have no idea how many pages my notebooks cover, these black-bound volumes in which I give substance to my days.

So, which work is more important, is it the novels or the notebooks?

I think it's the notebooks.

It's the notebooks that keep my daily writing up, which develop my style, because I'm always writing, every day, everywhere; I subject my writing to a new day, a new place, or the same place, day after day.

I attempt to write as quickly and directly as possible, without worrying about whether it's bad or good, without correcting or deleting, without troubling about whether it will be read; and it's here I achieve a vital freedom, I can write whatever I want.

If I only wrote novels, that freedom would atrophy, my writing would stagnate, my style would vanish; I'd be finished as a writer, I'm certain of it.

Tuesday 4 May

All my days are the same.

I do the same thing each and every day. I think it's this monotony which makes my books so dissimilar.

I do the same thing each and every day. I must remain still to set my books in motion.

I do the same thing each and every day. Get out of bed the same way as yesterday, alone the same way as tomorrow.

I do the same thing each and every day. In the past, only a few weeks ago, when there were several of us in the house, these dull days of mine were sometimes ruined, that did me good.

I do the same thing each and every day. I roll towards her side of the bed, but she isn't there.

I do the same thing each and every day. I don't listen to the radio, don't watch television, I read the papers and a few selected books, the same books, over and over again.

I do the same thing each and every day. I read Emily Dickinson over and over again, each and every day.

I do the same thing each and every day. Before, I used to write political pieces for the local press, I've written a political novel, it didn't change anything; now I do the same thing each and every day, I write, I do it each and every day.

Wednesday 5 May

I work, that's what I do each and every day.

When I'm not writing a novel, and when I'm not writing my notebooks, I translate the work of others, just now it's Gertrude Stein.

Thursday 6 May

I don't go anywhere, I'm not going anywhere, don't want to go anywhere; I can't face being here.

Some days, like today, I can't write a single sentence, not even a word. But still I sit at my writing table most of the day. I sit and wait. Wait for the words. Wait for the language. I wait for her to phone. But she doesn't. We used to talk every day; we could lie talking far into the night, and then carry on the next morning. I haven't spoken to her now for more than a week. It's not natural. I'll never get used to it, that I won't be speaking to her again.

This silence. What does she fill it with? Now the lamp on the writing table has begun to flicker, the bulb is fighting for its life. One, two, three slow flickers, then faster and faster, a heart beating, quicker and quicker until the light goes out.

I run upstairs, quickly get a new bulb from the kitchen cupboard. Sprint rapidly back down to the basement, feverishly replace the old bulb with the new one.

Each time I switch on the lamp, I get the urge to write. Shouldn't it be possible to find a new girlfriend? No, it's not possible. Not when you've loved.

In a letter I tell her: I find it hard to imagine you with anyone but me, and it's even harder to imagine myself with anyone but you.

Friday 7 May

I sleep with my mobile phone on my chest. It's the closest I get to her.

Only three weeks ago she rang and said: I'll be a bit late for dinner. I should have been happy, grateful, but at the time I was irritated, angry almost, it was Friday and I was waiting for her with dinner. Today is Friday, and I'm eating alone. It must be one of the worst things about loneliness: eating with someone who isn't there, every single day.

I've almost stopped eating, or I eat fast, always poor-quality processed food, I finish quickly. I eat so fast I've no time to think about the times we ate together.

We always bought three bottles of wine, drank two of them, now I drink all three bottles alone.

We ate, had the wine, and then we made love; I can't bear to think about it.

There are some difficult moments in *Tender Buttons*, this is one of them:

> A time to eat.
>
> A pleasant simple habitual and tyrannical and authorized and educated and resumed and artic-ulate separation.
>
> This is not tardy.

Sunday 9 May

No days are holidays.

Wake up in the living room, on the floor, close to Janne's sofa. I begged her to leave it here; the sofa and the lamps and as many of her things as possible, she left them.

Everything in here is as it used to be. I wake up on the floor, I've had too much wine. Three litres, that means that I've got one wine box left; I get some white bread from the kitchen, dip it in a glass of wine, eat.

Eat, drink.

It's simple, it's pure.

White bread, white body.

So simple, so pure.

Dip the bread in the wine; the way the bread fills itself with her blood.

The red, soft bread. Her red, full mouth; I consume it.

So red, so pure. So red, so white. So white, so pure. So white. So white, so white. So pure, so red.

So red, so dead, so born. So born and soft. So soft and sweet. So sweet-sweet. So sweet-red. So sweet-born in my mouth.

So dead-soft in my mouth. Inside it. Inside my mouth. In mine. So stillborn in my mouth. Inside. In my mouth. In my mouth inside.

In my mouth in mine. Inside. Inside my mouth. Now she's inside my mouth.

Now she's mine.

So simple, so pure.

Drink, eat.

Every day's a holiday.

Sunday 16 May

Haven't written for a week. Haven't washed for a week, I'm completely clean. Getting cleaner and cleaner.

Unshaven, dirty, like nature, that's total purity.

Thinner now, I've lost four kilos. Thinner, lighter, it's more difficult to move.

Throw up almost everything edible, except for the white bread.

Cut the electricity to the bell by the door; two thin wires in an arm, a quick, hard cut across the power arteries—now no one will answer a ring at the door.

Lie in bed the whole day, smoking and drinking. The way the daylight drains from the bedroom, the light runs out of the wound in the windowsill. A small moment of happiness? At last it's dark. Switch on the bedside lamp. The ashtrays and photos on the bedside table. The pens and notebooks. The cigarettes and flowers. The glasses and bottles on the floor. The bed is littered with books. Clothes. A clock radio under the pillow. Matches, paper, all this to compensate for an absence.

She slept with her nightie crumpled up over her knees, up over her thighs, up over her sex, up over her belly, up over her breasts. She slept with her nightie coiled around her neck in a white noose that wanted to throttle her.

You could tie her feet and arms; she would still be free.

She didn't know it, but she was never mine.

Monday 17 May

Independence Day. The worst day of the year; pure joy, pure violence, eating white bread, drinking her blood.

Eating white bread, swallowing it with red wine.

Stay in bed, fall asleep, wake up on the floor.

I've hit my head on the floor. She'll end up beating me to death.

Plaster on the cut. Put on a suit and white shirt, a dark tie. Black shoes. Go down to the basement. Turn on the television. Light a cigarette. Drink the dregs of some spirits. Like throwing petrol on the flames—watch John Huston's version of *Under the Volcano*.

Recall suddenly that the novel is somewhere in the house. Search the shelves, the plastic sacks in the basement store. The cupboards, the attic, find the book in Janne's wardrobe, in a box. *Under the Volcano* by Malcolm Lowry.

Geoffrey's letter to Yvonne: Come back, come back. I will stop drinking, anything. I'm dying without you. For Christ Jesus' sake, Yvonne, come back to me, hear me, it is a cry, come back to me, Yvonne, if only for a day . . .

Tuesday 18 May

'No se puede vivir sin amar.'

Do you remember, Janne, how the male owl shrieked, just outside our bedroom window, from the tree where it perched, an ominous shriek, the owl's cry in the night. We heard it and clutched each other. The owl that shrieked for her. The owl has gone. I can still hear its cry.

That owl is me.

That owl is me. Shrieking.

Can't live without love.

Wednesday 19 May

A broken heart is an illness.

Crying, vomiting, sweating, fits of anger, as if everything inside wants to come out.

Sleeplessness, fever. Nightmares, pangs of jealousy, as if everything outside wants to come in.

And she wants to come in.

TOMAS ESPEDAL

Down.

Chew her hair. Get hair in my throat.

Wash her hair down with wine.

And she enters me.

Friday 21 May

Those lovely hands, big, like working hands. Those short fingers; I swallow them.

Put her fingers down my throat.

I've lost six kilos. Getting slimmer and handsomer, younger and younger.

It's morning, it's evening.

Lie on the floor. That's happiness of a sort, too.

Feel the chill. Cold. Frost on the window, no steam, no sun, no light, so white, cold so early, winter so early, no spring.

Everything so early. Inside and out. The living room full of birds. In clusters, no, lines, in lines along the edges of the table, chair backs, pelmet, on the lamps, cheek by jowl on the floor, next to each other, squashed up close to each other, in lines, no clusters, in clusters on the floor, so together.

Such a tangled intermingling so interwoven.

Is the living room still filled with flowers?

Ah, the amaryllises which are too heavy for themselves.

The lilies which are too white.

The chrysanthemums which live too long.

The orchids that you left behind, fluttering their wings.

And the bushes of pink roses that you bought, they refuse to die. Why don't they fade away?

Why don't the flowers fade, is it the cold, the cold in the living room that gives the flowers artificial life?

The cold, no, the heat, the light, no, the darkness?

And the neighbours, what will they say? One would think you were trying to kill me with flowers.

Send me where you want.

Saturday 22 May

A lovely, sunny day. It has hung itself up like a picture outside the bedroom window; I don't believe in pictures any more.

I can't believe anything I see. I see you every single day. In the bathroom, in the living room, on the sofa, in the kitchen; it's not true that you've gone now you're gone. The truth is rather that you've moved back here in a malicious way.

So I must live with you.

Live with you whether you want to or not, if I want to or not, if you're here or not.

Sunday 23 May

I don't trust my eyes, or my ears; I heard you yesterday.

I don't trust my ears, or my eyes, or my hands either; they still hold you.

Everything in the house, in my entire body, behaves as if you're still here; is it just me that knows you've gone?

Not even sleep knows you've left.

Every night I sleep with you.

One night I suddenly sat up in bed. At last you'd come home. I'd been waiting for you, you'd been at a party with some girlfriends. I heard you on the stairs. Or did the tread give to a remembered pressure? I leapt out of bed and ran into the hall, banged my head as hard as I could against the stair.

I'd like to nail the doors shut. They open and close, they bang open and slam shut; its the draught and the wind that whistles through the house, lively and strong as you.

You're sending me down.

Down to the bottom.

Home to home.

At last I'm home.

There's no one here.

Monday 24 May

The great tits are here. The bullfinches are here. The yellowhammers are here. And the greenfinches are here. The blue tits are here, and here is the blackbird. The blackbird is here. The redpolls are here. The birds are here, males and females. My neighbour has nailed up a cat-shaped bird table in the birch tree outside the kitchen window. A black cat holding out a tray of birdseed. On the tray is written in large, painted words: FREE BIRDSEED.

My neighbour is in hospital. He had a fall in his living room. His wife found him, lying on the floor. She heard a crash in the living room, as if someone had fallen, there was no likelihood of his falling, but she ran down the stairs and found him lying on the floor.

I wish it had been me.

That someone had found me lying on the floor. That I had a wife who found me lying on the floor. That you found me lying on the floor. But I don't fall.

It's unbelievable that I don't fall, that I'm not stretched out on the floor. But I don't fall; I stagger around the living room doing all I can to keep myself upright.

Michelle Porte relates that Marguerite Duras could drink up to five litres of wine a day. Duras could hardly walk, she steadied herself on chairs and tables, and that was how she limped, like a dog with only three legs, around her living room.

In a small piece in her book *Practicalities* entitled 'Alcohol', Marguerite Duras wrote: 'As soon as I began drinking I became an alcoholic. Immediately I drank like an alcoholic. I forgot about everything. I started drinking in the evening, then I drank in the middle of the day, then in the morning, then I began to drink at night.'

Yann Andréa got Duras into hospital. In hospital Duras had seizures and hallucinations: 'Precisely ten thousand tortoises were ranged around the roof, in rows, like books. When evening came, they returned to their places beneath the eaves. It took several hours for the tortoises to get ready for the night, to slide into place next to each other. I was incensed that nature was so poorly organized.'

Yann Andréa was Duras's partner and lover; he was thirty-eight years her junior.

In *The Lover* Duras tells the story of how, as a fifteen-year-old girl, she began an affair with an older Chinese man. The novel was a sales success, a sensation. What would have happened if it had been the man telling the same story: the older man writing about his relationship with the young girl?

Why not write a despicable book?

The night Duras died, I dreamt about her. I've never told anyone about it, because it seems strange and conceited in a way, but I'd gone to bed after a row with Monica; I lay awake and couldn't sleep. Finally, as morning approached, I fell asleep. I dreamt about Duras. Confusing her with my mother. When I awoke and switched on the radio as usual, I heard on the news that Marguerite Duras was dead.

So what did it mean?

Nothing.

Duras resembled my mother, that was all. Duras was small, so was my mother. Duras smoked innumerable cigarettes, my mother did too. My mother had the same wrinkled face as Duras, she had the same unattractive beauty. My mother was very keen on clothes and jewellery; she always wore that ostentatious wrist watch, and all those rings and the gold bangles up her arms and necklaces and all the gaudy finery that Duras went in for. They had the same glasses. The same hands. My mother was a secretary; she always said she could write better than me.

Tuesday 25 May

A letter in the mail box. It's from Janne. She writes: I'm so scared I may have ruined your life.

Things are no easier just because Janne is a good person. The best person I know. There's no harm in her. Perhaps it would have been easier if she'd done something wrong, something rotten, something that was bad, but she isn't like that. She's left me, that's all.

Of necessity, she writes. She is young, I was her first lover, there's so much she wants to see, so much she must experience, just as you've done, she writes.

Things weren't even between us, she writes. You've had several partners, there's so much you've done, and I've hardly done anything, she writes.

That dreadful age gap, she writes.

In my own way I'll always love you, she writes.

The letter doesn't make things easier, it makes everything more difficult.

I fold the letter and put it in my jacket pocket. I walk into the city. It's a fifty-minute hike. It's one of the loveliest walks I know; today I take the coastal route and not the mountain route into town.

Shop at the Off Licence. Put the wine boxes in my pack and pay a visit to the Angel's record shop, buy the new one from Kurt Wagner and Lambchop. The Angel says: Have you grown a mourning beard and become a dosser?

Mourning beard.

That's almost exactly what it is.

Ah, Einar, I've got a broken heart, I say.

It's when it's cured you'll have to worry, he says.

Is that possible? Or is that just a form of words, a saw, a lie?

Look after yourself, he says.

The Angel's an important person in town, because his presence here makes a big difference. If he wasn't here, the town would be colder, harder, nastier.

Perhaps he's right. The worst is when the broken heart begins to mend. But my broken heart won't mend; I'm certain of it.

Friday 28 May, evening, Øyjordsveien
So the house is empty.

The house is empty and clean and quiet.

I've finally got that furniture of hers, ours, out of the house. Out with the sofa. Out with the dining table. Out with the chairs, carpets. Out with the bed we slept in. Out with the lamps and books. Out with the clothes she left behind; out with the dresses and stockings and shoes; it was as if she was leaving me for a second time.

Now there's nothing to make a disturbance in the house, no flowers, no lamps, no dresses, no shoes that tramp the stairs at night. No smells, no clothes to clutch in the cupboard. No trace of her, not even a hair. Everything has been washed and tidied, slung out and smashed. One could say that the house has been returned to its initial state, the way it was before we moved in, before anyone moved in, the house has been returned to its original emptiness.

A window in the bedroom that won't close; it's always been open, first during my father and mother's time, then with Janne and me, no one shut the bedroom window, and now it's too late, the window won't close. Apart from the window that won't close, and a few dents and marks on the bathroom door from rows and kicks, the house is pretty much the same as it was before we lived in it.

Empty and beautiful.

It's a beautiful house. Not too large, a little house in a terrace of four. Small rooms, antiquated, presumably, as the neighbours have torn down some of their partitions and opened the houses up. But our house has kept its small rooms: a small living room, a small kitchen, three small bedrooms, a narrow bathroom, as if a small family lived here.

A small family did live here. The family got smaller and smaller; now there's only one person living in the house.

The little house has got too large for him; he's emptied all the rooms and shut them up, all except one.

He sleeps and works in the basement room.

He writes in the basement. Just at this moment he could swear there's the sound of someone upstairs, at the door, calling Papa down to him. He turns down the music, hears nothing and begins to cry.

Saturday 29 May

He's been with his daughter for nineteen years. She needs to move, move out and find her own flat, her own space. She needs to find independence, her own life, but for her father it's a huge sadness being separated from his daughter; he loves and needs her, but she needs something else, something more than him.

It's a shock for the father when his daughter moves out.

Even though he's prepared for her moving out one day, that she must, that it's natural for a daughter to move away from her father, that it's not natural for her to live with him for the length of time he'd like, it's still a shock for the father when his daughter moves out. And the next day, when she doesn't come home as usual, when she doesn't call down to him in the basement as usual, he sits there all day completely paralysed in his chair, he doesn't know what to do or how he can cope without her.

A man of almost fifty who's deserted by his daughter; what's he to do, how is he to occupy himself?

Without his daughter.

Without my daughter. Each time I write my, I think of how little we possess; we own nothing.

Not our children, not our parents or family, not our history, not even our childhood, adolescence, friends, girlfriends, not our lover or love itself; we own nothing.

Sunday 30 May

It's cold inside the house, outside it's warm, it's spring outside, winter inside. Been drinking every day for almost two months; it's the only pleasant thing now, getting fuddled, getting drunk. A certain warmth in inebriation, like pissing in your pants.

A certain presence in intoxication, as if they're all still here, the living and the dead, in the house, or perhaps you just don't notice they're gone.

A certain warmth, a certain presence, a certain joy, as when you drink wine and feel that she really is there in your body, she's taken up abode in your body, that she still lives inside your body.

Pains around my heart—too many cigarettes, too much alcohol, but the pains vanish when I drink.

Can't eat properly, sleep badly, don't shower, don't tidy up, don't clean, the dirt gathers, in the house, on my body. Where's that smell coming from; from outside, from inside, like the smell of stagnant water, it's become difficult to move.

TOMAS ESPEDAL

Who should I move for?

My hair lengthens, my beard grows. It's become hard to move in all this dirt, in the detritus that gathers like fallen leaves on the basement floor, six feet underground; this is where I live, it's almost like living in the wild.

Monday 31 May

Is this how it happens—that age comes one night when you're lying in bed alone, suddenly, like a shadow in the room; it lays itself over you, pushes you down into the bed, holds your head in a terrible grip and breathes ice into your mouth. A chill that spreads throughout you body. That blows out your ardour and warmth from inside; a thin layer of frost around your lungs and heart, around your stomach and liver, around your lymph system and testicles. You are cold. You wake up and you're cold. The ice has cut its way through your face. Tiny cuts around your eyes and mouth; the way the skin on your face has stiffened. A cold face. Cold and heavy hands. The ice has sliced off your genitals. You wake up and have lost your spark, your heat, you've lost your belief, strength, you've lost your desire.

You've lost the ability to love.

You can't do it, you can't love anyone again.

It's the end.

You say the end, but love doesn't want to end.

Notes

The Abélard quotations are from 'The Correspondence of Abélard and Héloïse—with an excerpt from the works of Abélard' (*Brevvekslingen mellom Abélard og Héloïse—med et utdrag fra Abélards verker*, Aschehoug, 2002), translated by Harald Gullichsen.

The Ovid poem is from Thea Selliaas Thorsen's retelling of 'Ars amandi—The Art of Loving' (*Ars amandi—Kunsten å elske*, Gyldendal, 2006).